MARTYRS, HEROES, AND FOOLS

MARTYRS, HEROES, AND FOOLS

A novel

by

JOHN WELLS

Adelaide Books
New York/Lisbon
2018

MARTYRS, HEROES, AND FOOLS
A novel
By John Wells

Published by Adelaide Books, New York / Lisbon
adelaidebooks.org

Editor-in-Chief
Stevan V. Nikolic

For any information, please address Adelaide Books
at info@adelaidebooks.org

or write to:

Adelaide Books
244 Fifth Ave. Suite D27
New York, NY, 10001

ISBN-13: 978-1-949180-42-8
ISBN-10: 1-949180-42-5

Printed in the United States of America

Content

1.

Nagasaki, Japan, 1944

Naniko can't sit still. She fidgets, she squirms, she drums her fingers on the desk. The dismissal bell is five minutes late, and if it doesn't ring soon she'll be late for work. Her shift at the munitions factory begins precisely thirty minutes after school lets out, and her supervisor is as strict about tardiness as her schoolmaster. One minute late, he docks an hour's pay, and sometimes he singles you out at one of his meetings and calls you an unpatriotic shirker. The bell rings; Naniko stands, bows courteously to the teacher, grabs her backpack, and bolts for the door.

The factory makes cartridges for the Imperial Army's infantry rifles. The work is vital to the war effort, and government officials hold frequent meetings to explain how critical rifle ammunition is to the Army. The officials set quotas. If the quotas are met, they heap praise, but if the quotas fall short, they chastise the workers and schedule more lectures. During the early days of the war, Naniko's shift rarely missed quota, but now shortages of critical primers or casings or bullets or gunpowder cause them to fall short. Even so, the officials blame the workers. It isn't fair, but they do it anyway.

As she's taking her place in the production line (Thank goodness she isn't late after all) she's relieved to find they have everything they need, so making quota won't be difficult. She finds the hand loading operation easy enough to establish a steady rhythm: Set the primer in the loading machine, position the cartridge case, pour gunpowder into the casing, set the lubricated bullet, and pull the handle to crimp the casing and eject the completed round. It might not be difficult, but it's monotonous: set, position, measure and pour, pull, eject; set, position, measure and pour, pull, eject, etc., for hours on end.

Monotonous or not, each step is critical. During one of the lectures an official explained what could happen if a rifle round isn't made properly. The danger comes from not pouring the prescribed amount of gunpowder: Too much in a cartridge makes a rifle barrel burst when it's fired, and it's just as bad if there's not enough—a "short round" it's called. When fired, there won't be enough pressure to make the bullet clear the barrel and it becomes an obstruction. Then the next time the soldier fires his rifle, the barrel explodes. Either way the result's the same: One of the Emperor's brave soldiers is maimed or even killed just as though he's shot by the enemy.

"Any problems?" she asks the bitchy old babaa she relieves.

"Primers again. We ran out of primers and had to wait for over an hour for primers," the old hag complains. "But you shouldn't have any worry. They found plenty for your shift."

Naniko settles down and begins work. She prides herself in her meticulous care. She vows not to do the work of the enemy. She knows if she's careless, she might be the cause of some soldier—maybe even be her cousin Hideio serving in the Philippines—to become a victim of one of her bullets. Regardless, during the seventh hour of her shift while she lets her mind wonder why the schoolmaster was late ringing the dismissal bell, she sets the primer, mistakenly pours only a quarter measure of gunpowder into a cartridge case, sets the bullet, pulls the lever, and ejects a "short round." It goes into a crate of ammunition consigned to the army garrison on Okinawa, where it is destined to play a pivotal role in a soldier's life.

2.

China, 1944

Honor is the soul of Bushido. Courage, duty, and integrity are important, but honor is foremost. In keeping with Bushido, everything in Captain Takeo Kuroki's early life prepared him to be an officer in the Imperial Army, but right now he's not living up to the spirit. Keeping his mind focused on this senseless mission, a routine patrol among these stinking hills of Shandong Province, is difficult. He's been out here in rural China since the war started, but now he's missing his chance to fight the Americans in the Pacific and win glory like his classmates at Zama. Every time he's put in for transfer, his colonel has forwarded them with a recommendation of refusal.

Yet, duty must be served and though it seems futile, he goes through the motions. Like his men he's sweaty, tired, and bored from marching break-step in column, raising dust and pollen and insects along country back roads for three days. Boring as it is, it has to be done, and now that it's finished, he's done his duty and tells his sergeant to let the men fall out. As standing orders prescribe, he goes immediately to report to his superior, the battalion commander, Colonel Watanabe.

The first time Takeo met the colonel, he recognized him as one of those political bastards who come to China—he loudly made no secret of it—for the benefit of his fitness report. It's necessary for a colonel to have commanded a battalion before being considered for promotion to brigadier general in charge of a division.

As Takeo is starting to make his report, he senses that the colonel is agitated, impatiently rubbing his hands together, anxious for Takeo to get on with it. Takeo obliges. Finished, he hears the colonel demand, "Well, whom do you know in Tokyo, Kuroki-san? Somebody on the Imperial General Headquarters Staff, perhaps?"

"Why, no one, sir," Takeo says. "I thought the colonel was aware that I'm not political. It's true that my grandfather was a samurai of the old school, but when he sided with those who went against Emperor Meiji, he was dismissed from the Army. Most of his comrades committed seppuku, but he never did. He saw his duty to help my father raise me in the ways of the samurai. When it was time for me to go to the military academy at Zama, he had to call in debts from old acquaintances. Even so, there were some senior officers who wanted to see me dismissed, but because I was the academy's kendo champion, they failed. Oh, no sir, I know no one of consequence in Tokyo, and certainly no member of the IGHQ."

"Then how do you explain these?" Watanabe asks, plunking down an opened envelope upon his desk.

"Sir?"

"They're orders, Kuroki-san. Your orders transferring you to a new duty station," Watanabe stammers.

"I'm sure that the colonel is aware that several times I've put in for transfer to the Pacific Theatre where I can fight the Americans," Takeo states.

"I am indeed aware of it. And each time I've forwarded your request with my recommendation for refusal. I need you here in China. It seems like I've been overruled and I'd like to know why," the colonel complains.

"I have no idea, sir," Takeo asserts.

"Well, at least I'm happy that you haven't gone behind my back."

"May I ask where, sir?"

"Where? Oh, yes, of course. You're going to the Thirty-second Imperial Army. You're also promoted to major. You've been selected to be aide de camp to the commanding general of the Thirty-second Army, Major General Mitsuru Ushijimi. I suppose congratulations are in order, but I'm sorry to lose you."

"But where's the Thirty-second Army, sir?" Takeo asks.

"Why, on Okinawa, Major Kuroki," Watanabe answers, "You're going to fight the Americans on Okinawa."

3.

Tokyo, 1945

The winter gripping Japan in January is unusually bitter. Nights in central Honshu are starless for weeks on end and dawns arrive as gray events in a frigid world without sunshine and color. The weather is relentless, but now an artic air mass drifts out of Manchuria and settles down for a spell over the island nation. Blasts of bitterly cold winds blow mists from the mountains, ice the trees, and bare Mount Fuji in all her perfection. After enduring weeks of relentless fire bombings in burned-out Tokyo, shivering Nihon-jin pray to their sacred mountain for blessed relief.

In the finest room of the small inn reserved for visiting dignities in Tokyo's Government Section, a hawk-faced samurai stirs beneath the warm blanket covering his slender body and breathes in the morning air. Despite the early hour a jochu-san has minutes before crept in to slide away the double set of shoji shutters and let the chill morning air cleanse the staleness of the night, the smell of troubled sleep.

For all the jochu-san's attempted stealth, his presence hasn't gone unnoticed. For more than an hour, even while the flickering candles of the stone toro lanterns in the garden were fast losing their power to the growing dawn, the occupant of the room has been feigning sleep in a losing fight. Try as he might he's been unable to go back to sleep. Habits rigidly formed will not yield. The invasion by the jochu-san is nothing more than a summons to rise.

General Mitsuru Ushijimi props himself upon an elbow and gazes beyond the opened shoji at Mount Fuji-san's show. Perhaps, he ponders, there's truth to the old myth that Fuji-san can bring good luck. Could there be factual basis to the mystical aspects of life, or was it all just hopeful folklore? He doubts it, but just maybe the American bombers will not fly today.

"You're dreaming, Mitsuru-san," he mutters to himself before he heaves a sigh and forces himself to rise from the snug futon. Shivering, he makes a futile attempt to stir life into the dormant charcoal in the kotatsu urn.

"Damn that lazy jochu-san," he curses, but quickly decides to go without warmth. He's used to it. Pulling himself to full height, he stretches his stiff muscles before striding to the far side of the room, where he extracts his sword from its scabbard, squats, and begins his morning exercise regimen, a series of leaps and shouts and slashes in the air to dispatch phantom enemies as he's done every morning for over ten thousand awakenings. With perspiration dripping from the corners of his pencil-thin mustache, he's ready to begin his day.

Morning toilet is another routine, and soon he finds himself starring at his lathered image in the shaving mirror. Troubled eyes return his gaze, and images from recollection of the events of yesterday when he appeared before the IGHQ to give them a formal briefing about his preparations for defending Okinawa from the American invasion everyone knows is coming.

In the big picture of what is facing the Empire, the war is following an entirely different scenario than what Prime Minister Tojo predicted. Yet, nobody—especially members of the

IGHQ—is allowed to criticize. Lord Tojo based his decision to go to war with the United States on the premise that it would end in stalemate. Japan needed resources and war was the only way to get them. While it was a given that Japan could not compete with America's industrial might, it was thought that their isolationist policy made them hesitant and unprepared to go to war. At the onset of hostilities, Japan would defeat them at every encounter, so soon they would tire of this humiliation and accept an armistice, leaving most of Japanese gains intact.

It wasn't turning out that way. To be sure, there was early success, but all that changed. Momentum shifted, beginning when the Imperial Navy suffered a humiliating defeat at the Battle of Midway. This was followed by the debacle at Guadalcanal in the Solomon Islands. It was the beginning of a series of stinging defeats until it's now plain that Lord Tojo's grand strategy is fatally wrong.

When the Americans invaded the Philippines, the IGHQ realized that the next step will be invasion of the home islands. Last August the General Staff gave Ushijimi command of the garrison on Okinawa and told him to turn the island into an invincible bastion. They promised him nine months to complete the job, but General Yamashita's defeat in the Philippines changed the timetable. Last week they sent a message ordering him to come to Tokyo and brief them of his strategy, tactics, logistics, and order of battle.

Obey, of course. He flew back to Tokyo and without even taking a single day off to visit his wife, went straight away to headquarters and began his briefing. It consumed the better part of two days, concluding yesterday afternoon.

This morning finds him ready to return to Okinawa along with his new aide Major Kuroki. Now dressed, he throws his few personal belongings in his suitcase and looks around the room before preparing to leave. He buckles his sword belt, dons his skullcap, slides away the shoji shutters, and strides forward into the hallway where Kuroki-san should be waiting to attend him. Mitsuru smiles; Kuroki-san is there, handsome and athletic and dressed neat as a pin.

"Sir, yes sir!" Major Kuroki shouts and snaps to rigid attention the instant the shoji opens. He salutes, bows, and does not smile in his formal greeting.

Ushijimi bites his lip to keep from laughing at his aide's outlandish display of protocol. He's been hoping that his new aide will be circumspect in day-to-day interaction, and his first impression is favorable. Kuroki-san was attentive when he met his new commander as Mitsuru was debarking from the plane when it landed at Hadena. Mitsuru's first concern was whether the major had taken leave before reporting for duty. He had not.

"Go home, Major," Ushijimi him. "Visit your family and unwind for a spell. Come back in three days and be ready to assume your new duties."

Ushijimi remembers how Major Kuroki smiled and thanked him, but didn't leave until he had taken possession of the small suitcase and promised to deliver it to his quarters. That was his last sight of Kuroki-san, and in the evening everything was done.

Now he's finding the major's promptness another reason to be satisfied. But from experience, he knows it will take several weeks for the major to get used to his superior's relaxed way of dealing with subordinates. On the other side of the coin, he hopes his new aide won't give cause to see his stern discipline when it comes to slackers.

As Ushijimi takes leave of his room, his orderly Yoshio-san rushes in to retrieve his general's suitcase and take it to the staff car waiting to transport them to Hadena Airport. On an impulse, Ushijimi decides to forego taking breakfast in the VIP lounge and leads the way to the main dining hall. If the major is surprised, he hides his feelings.

"Were you able to go home without difficulty, Kuroki-san?" Ushijimi asks while waiting to be served.

"Hai, domo," Kuroki responds. "The train is running without interruption."

"And your parents? I trust they're all right and were surprised to see you. I'm sorry that you were unable to tell them about your visit beforehand."

"They're both well and very pleasantly surprised," Takeo answers. "They sent their thanks, as do I, sir. My visit was most unexpected."

"Think nothing of it, Major."

"Arrigato, General Ushijimi-chan."

"Were you able to do anything special?"

"Indeed, we did," Kuroki explains. "I took Mother to Kamakura to visit the Daibutsu Buddha. She said a prayer and insists that I tell you she's going to say a prayer for you every day until we win the war and everyone is safely home."

"I am honored," Ushijimi says. "You must tell her I say arrigato when you write."

Takeo smiles and nods.

"You graduated from the Zama Academy, did you not?" the general asks.

"That's correct, sir."

"And your sword? It has the look of ageless quality about it? May I ask about it?" Mitsuru explores.

"An heirloom, sir. It belonged to my grandfather. He gave it to me when I graduated," Takeo explains.

"You were close to your grandfather?"

"Very close, sir."

"Obviously he was a samurai warrior, was he not?"

"Yes, sir. Of the old school," Takeo answers.

17

Ushijimi smiles and abandons the subject—for the time being, even as he makes a mental note to delve more into Kuroki's background later.

Breakfast over, the automobile trip to the airport is made in silence. When they arrive, they board a transport plane, which is warmed up and waiting to take off. Aloft, they circle Fuji-san once for good luck, with each man looking at the sacred mountain as though it's probably the last time he'll see it.

The plane settles on a southwesterly course. Ushijimi peers out the window at the billowing clouds and the white-capped sea. Silently he allows his mind delve back into the briefing he'd given the General Staff. The one charade is that nobody will admit the war is lost. During his briefing Ushijimi plays the game and hides his apprehension. The IGHQ can't deal with apprehension, especially in their senior officers. Blind optimism is what they demand, and so blind optimism is what they get.

What he tells them is that he intends to defend Okinawa in classic warfare. He bases this strategy on the realistic assessment that once the battle begins, he can't be reinforced. The enemy has shown that when they invade, they seal off the area and sweep the seas clean of Japanese ships.

The members of the IGHQ frowned. It's a hard truth to face. He went on to defend his strategy by explaining lessons learned from experience in the Pacific. "We have to face facts," he told them. "The Americans have developed such skill in amphibious operations that now they can land whenever and wherever they chose. Time after time we've tried without success to prevent them from coming ashore, so why expend valuable troops in trying to stop them? I don't intend to make the same mistake."

"So your plan is to let them come ashore without a fight?"

"Yes," he told them. "After they commit their entire force, I am going to engage them in classic infantry warfare. They'll obviously attack our impregnable defenses, and I'll defeat them, drive them back into the sea, and destroy them. With such a devastating loss, the Americans will have no choice but to sue for peace."

At the conclusion of his briefing, the General Staff rose to their feet and informed him that Emperor Hirohito, the Son of Heaven, has decided to honor him. In August, seven months hence, he will be promoted to full general.

"Arrigato," Ushijimi said, bowing. "I shall try to be worthy of such honor."

Members of the General Staff nodded and smiled their approval. Their chosen man was proving to be an excellent choice to lead the Thirty-second Imperial Army.

Now, as he is flying back to Okinawa, Mitsuru is consumed with one thought: August? Will it ever come?

4.

Okinawa, 1945

There isn't any soldier in any army who'll disagree with Major Kuroki's opinion that generals' aides are nothing more than glorified jochu-sans—pretty boys in pretty uniforms with pretty aiguillettes draped over their shoulders while wearing pretty medals they've neither earned nor deserved. The universal opinion is they're snobbish bastards enjoying fancy privileges that officers of lesser rank can only dream about. In short order, Takeo finds out this just isn't so.

Now he finds himself immersed in a world where all these fancy privileges are earned by hard work and long hours, days and nights running together, all the while overwhelmed by demanding tasks in which his contributions are more important than he'd ever imagined. As an aide he's expected to be an extension of his general's eyes, ears, voice, and often even his mind. To his delight his duties are far more interesting than anything he's ever done before. He sits at the focal point of all decision-making, privy to everything that's happened, is happening, or about to happen on Okinawa.

On the other hand, his original opinion is spot on. There are times when he's just a glorified jochu-san. The thing is, it's enjoyable.

The big downside in his hectic life is that he doesn't know enough about the garrison to perform consistently at the level his superior needs. Lacking background knowledge, he finds himself struggling under an onerous load.

General Ushijimi is sympathetic, but he knows how to bring his aide up to speed. "I want you to drop everything else and concentrate on one assignment," Ushijimi tells him. "Don't worry about your other duties. For the time being, I want you to concentrate on three subjects and prepare a private report, which you'll give to me and nobody else. The three subjects are: (1.) Okinawa and its people, (2.) the Order of Battle, and (3.) the strengths and weaknesses of my staff officers."

"How soon do you want it, sir?"

Finding the question impertinent, Ushijimi answers "As soon as possible. Do it quickly, but do it well. Just do it, do it, do it!"

"Hai domo. Yes, sir!" Takeo answers, bows, and off he goes.

The first subject he finds in an encyclopedia. A map shows Okinawa, largest island of the Ryukus, sprawling across the South China Sea in a southwesterly direction for about a hundred kilometers. To expand this basic knowledge, he tours the island and discovers a gentle land with gentle people enjoying gentle weather most of the year. Spring is the rainy season, when storms and typhoons turn the island into a muddy quagmire. The island has three distinct areas: the northern wilderness, the isthmus, and the southern plateau. Each part is different from the others, and the whole is different from any of its parts. The north is wilderness with its coast dominated by fishing villages. It narrows abruptly to form Ishikawa, an isthmus dominated by sandy beaches. One in particular, Hagushi Beach seems ideal for amphibious landings. He understands why General Ushijimi believes the enemy will land here. The third area is the south, a plateau of farmland where most Okinawans live. In shape, it's an inverted triangle with the base dominated by hills called Kakazu Ridge. At the center of these hills stands Shuri Castle, the ancient bastion that guards the south. Nearby is the seaport and capital city Naha.

The second part of his assignment is just as easy. As aide, has access to the 32nd Army organization charts along with detailed maps and construction plans. But here he finds a problem and it comes from the IGHQ's interference. They're constantly stripping Ushijimi's garrison of seasoned troops and assigning them to the Philippines or Formosa. Promises to send replacements never materialize. Takeo finds himself writing, "Despite the chaos caused by IGHQ interference, we can field over 110,000 men, but not all are experienced. The sad fact is that only 77,000 are regular Army; the other 33,000 are made up of sailors from the Imperial Navy and Okinawan Boetai home guard."

While the organization may be chaotic, their order of battle is not. After the Americans come ashore, the Thirty-second Army will fight a defensive battle from within an elaborate network of underground defenses constructed so that the enemy cannot attack one position without being subjected to devastating crossfire from supporting positions. Beneath Shuri Castle, headquarters is immune to artillery and aerial bombs.

If the first two parts of his assignment are easy, the final part is not. In assessing the effectiveness of General Ushijimi's staff means he has to delve into the personalities of senior staff officers. Of the staff as a whole, it's easy. But when it comes to expressing opinions about officers who are his seniors, it's a daunting task. But daunting or not, he's been given an assignment and is honor bound to be honest about what he thinks.

What he discovers is that the Staff lacks cohesiveness. They have no singleness of purpose, and the result is that they're ineffective! Clever men, to be sure, the staff is a collection of the most intelligent officers he's ever met. But clever or not, they're polarized around two opposing senior officers: Chief-of-Staff General Isamu Cho and Senior Operations Officer Colonel Hiromichi Harata. Bickering between Cho and Harata can affect the battle and cause disaster.

What to do? Even though he's honor bound to express an opinion, it has potential to ruin him. Takeo is undecided and mulls his options, but in the end he decides it's his sworn duty to make his views known. He decides to devout the entire third section of his report on the staff's polarization caused by these two officers. It means delving into their personalities. The first will be Cho, because he's senior and also the more volatile.

Takeo finds himself with two minds about Cho. The general's spent his entire career crashing, bashing, and smashing his way through reckless escapades. On one hand Takeo admires the man's aggressive sense of duty and on the other hand wonders why Cho hasn't been shot or at least stripped of rank and cashiered from the Army. While still a captain he joined in a plot to overthrow the Government, but when the Kempei Police foiled the plot, Cho went unpunished while his coconspirators went to prison. Then in 1938 Cho again thrust himself into high politics when without orders he attacked a Russian outpost in Manchurian, and even though Japan had to make a formal apology to avoid war, Cho suffered no consequence.

General Cho often acts delusional. He fancies himself the reincarnation of an ancient Samurai warrior and acts the part. When someone disagrees with him he shouts obscenities and bullies the man. But then suddenly he'll make an about face and bully officers who moments before supported him. One of his favorite tactics is to use his ivory-tipped cigarette holder as a sword of sorts to intimidate opponents. He drinks and becomes a mean and nasty drunk. To satisfy his insatiable lust, he keeps a concubine named Fumiko in his quarters. He calls her a geisha, but geisha she is not. She may be good looking and sultry, but she has the roving eye of a common whore, a yariman. In the end, Cho can be described as a man who loves women, loves whiskey, loves controversy, loves brawling, and hates the law. Violence is his solution to everything he considers wrong with the world.

In Colonel Harata, the Operations Officer, Takeo finds the other side of the coin. At first, Takeo has trouble determining Harata's exact nature because the colonel is a cultured man, artful in the ways of hiding his true nature, which ever so gradually emerges as a gentleness of spirit not found very often in this violent occupation of soldiering. He shows a social side, a considerate conversationalist, a perfect gentleman, a courteous host or guest. But let the subject of military tactics come up, a latent malevolence rises to expose his combative side, and he makes it clear he's either going to win you over or grind you down.

In summation, it's plain that Harata and Cho are incompatible and bound to clash. The reason is simple: In General Cho Hiromichi Harata finds everything he despises, and vice versa. They hate each other. In the final paragraph of his report, Takeo writes, "The result of their differences is that staff meetings are loud exchanges of shouts and insults. No matter who is right or wins the argument, the Staff is a house divided, with one half of the staff officers at odds with the other half. If this continues and we don't come together, I fear we are lost."

When the report is written and ready to submit, Takeo hesitates for two days before putting his name to it and another day before he has nerve enough to place it in his commander's in-box. Then he goes to his room and sits in silence, waiting to be summoned. His wait isn't long. Within minutes, Yoshio-san appears at his doorway and informs him that the general wants to see him immediately. Takeo meekly follows the orderly the few steps to Ushijimi's quarters.

He knocks on the door, enters and bows in silence. Ushijimi says nothing for almost a minute and then asks in metered tone of voice, "Kuroki-san, who in hell do you think you are?"

"Just a soldier doing his duty, sir," he says, feeling blood flush his face.

"Duty, you say?" thunders Ushijimi. "You think it's your duty to judge and insult the generals of the IGHQ for ordering troops in and out of my command?"

"I wrote only about their results of their actions that affect us, sir. I mean no disrespect regarding their intentions."

"I noticed that, Major," Ushijimi responds. "You're very clever with words."

"I try to be, sir."

"We'll let that go for now, but it's the third section of your report I want to discuss. It's anything but what I expected. You criticize—with definite disrespect, I might add—both of my chief assistants, General Cho and Colonel Harata. I see no clever words in this instance. Explain yourself, please."

Kuroki is prepared to answer the charge. The general's reaction is what Takeo has anticipated. "Sir, I agonized over every word in the report. I have great respect for both officers and their achievements, but I stand by my opinion. The damage they're creating with their arguments negates what they're trying to accomplish, sir."

After mulling his aide's answer, Ushijimi says "I see."

"As I said before, sir," Takeo says. "I considered it my duty. If my words constitute disrespect, I am sorry. I am, of course, junior to both officers, but I still have a soldier's experienced eye to recognize errant judgment. In my humble opinion, both officers are letting their dislike for one another overrule their objectivity. I suggest only that they need to step back and re-think their actions. If I am wrong, I apologize and am ready to suffer the consequences."

"There will be no consequences, Major," Ushijimi declares with a sigh. "Even if I thought there should be, there's no time to find a replacement for you. Good, bad or indifferent, we're stuck with each other."

"I'm sorry, sir."

"Don't be, Takeo-san. You only verify what I've been suspecting. About your overall performance, I'm well satisfied. I have just one immediate task."

"Sir?"

"Take this goddamned report along with any copies and all your notes, and burn the entire lot."

"As you wish, sir."

5.

Okinawa, 1945

Not one to let sores fester, Ushijimi knows he has to take immediate action to rid his staff of the problems pointed out in Kuroki-san's report. It may border on the impertinent, but it clearly discloses the idiotic conflict between Cho and Harata. It has to stop and stop immediately. He'll chastise both, and he decides to start with General Cho; he's the senior staff officer and over the years has shown himself to be an old friend who's like a faithful watchdog willing to grovel when the master's angry. Colonel Harata will be next. Before this day is done, there will be nothing but harmony on his staff.

"Isamu, what am I going to do with you?" Ushijimi begins when his chief of staff is standing before him. "Your conduct has become impossible. I find it hard to know where to begin."

The expression on Cho's face is total surprise. He can hardly believe his ears. The old man is obviously angry, treating him like a cadet. Cho's first thought is maybe Mitsuru-chan is letting the pressure of command get to him. But this just can't be. Regardless, Cho decides he'd better obey and accept whatever his commander has in mind. Remembering his days as a plebe at Zama, he braces up and stands at rigid attention, half expecting Mitsuru to tell him to stand at ease, agitated when he does not.

Pausing long enough to calm his emotions, Ushijimi begins. "First of all, Isamu-san," he says. "As a matter of principle, let me explain that what I'm about to say should not be considered a stain on your honor. In the spirit of our friendship, I'm asking this. But if you do not agree, we will be done with this, here and now."

Cho grimaces at the realization that Mitsuru has another option: He can order him to return to Tokyo on the next flight. This is no idle threat. He's known Mitsuru long enough to know that his stern sense of duty won't let him back down, even if it means that the consequences would mean any officer so dismissed would have to commit ritual seppuku. Cho sets his mouth, grits his teeth, and grunts agreement.

Even so, Cho is startled by Ushijimi's next words. "I know precisely what's going on in that samurai mind of yours, Isamu. You're thinking that there's only one way to settle this argument with Colonel Harata. You'll challenge him to a duel. We both can recall when the Emperor forbid dueling, feuds ended up in a kendo match in which both opponents are honor bound for the loser to commit seppuku. I know you well enough to know this is exactly what's going through your mind. Right?"

The words cause Cho's eyes to open wide. This is precisely the conclusion he's come to. Cho clinches his teeth and nods.

"I have a solution for that eventuality," Mitsuru continues. "If either you or Harata-san or the both of you even so much as allude to such an arrangement, I'll order the both of you home in disgrace immediately. Understand? Home—in—disgrace!"

Isamu feels his stomach muscles contract. The old man isn't bluffing.

"Let me explain it another way," Mitsuru goes on. "If you and Colonel Harata don't patch up your differences immediately, if you don't start working together in perfect harmony, if you don't become a team, then I will have no recourse except to order you both home. Have I made myself clear?"

"Hai, wakari mas," Cho responds with a bow.

"Dismissed," Ushijimi says in conclusion. "Colonel Harata is waiting outside. On your way out will you please inform him to enter. I have similar words for him."

Like Cho, Harata is receptive and promises to behave. If Mitsuru were a gambling man, he'd bet that the colonel's promise is the stronger of the two.

During February, things improve. There still may be gaged distance between Cho and Harata, but it seems to be closing. Ushijimi won't allow himself to believe he's achieved harmony, but staff unity seems to be on the mend. As February drifts into March, General Ushijimi is convinced he's achieved staff unity. It's timely; news comes from Tokyo that an American carrier fleet is prowling the East China Sea.

Suddenly the war is upon them. Enemy planes bomb Naha and its airfield. Invasion can come at any time. One morning they'll awaken to find the sea horizon filled with American ships. On the fourth of March Ushijimi instructs Cho to activate Thirty-second Army Headquarters in the bunker beneath Shuri Castle. The date has other significance: Tomorrow will be is Ushijimi's fifty-eighth birthday.

It's Cho who broaches the subject of a birthday party for his old friend, because no other officer would dare mention the subject. Ushijimi is notorious for his opposition of such nonsense. They're right—he would nip the idea in the bud.

"Oh, don't be a stick in the mud, Mitsuru," Cho argues. "The officers want to honor you, and I think you should let them."

"Stick in the mud or not, I don't approve of parties or displays of affection in the Army. Of all people you should know that."

"Maybe so, but there's another factor I think we should consider," Cho presses.

"Which is?"

"Their morale," Cho says. "These men realize that the Americans will soon be here, which means many loyal officers will die on this damned island. This party is probably their last chance to enjoy themselves."

Ushijimi frowns and knows he's going to give in. He nods his approval.

"Good show!" Cho says, laughing. "Besides we lots of whiskey in our storeroom and it'll probably end up being destroyed. We shouldn't let it go to waste, should we?"

"Damn you, Isamu," Ushijimi chuckles.

The staff is delighted with Cho's success, and to a man they pitch in to decorate the officers club. Preparation becomes a party in itself.

The evening shapes up as everything they envisioned. Before dinner pleasantries include western style libations. Despite the government's assertion about hating alcohol, Imperial Army officers have a fond taste for American liquor. The cocktail hour is brash, boisterous, loud, and uninhibited. While many officers get tipsy, leave it to Cho to down whiskey in such quantity that when the gong for dinner sounds, he's drunk, mean and nasty. He's completely out of his head shouting nonsense, cursing, slurring his words, and waving his arms like a windmill in a storm. It's all Ushijimi can do to convince him to come to the head table and sit for dinner. After several minutes of labored silence, Cho abandons his chair and staggers back to the bar for more whiskey.

Ushijimi glares at the empty chair before whispering to his aide, "I should have closed the damned bar when dinner was served. Please go watch him, Takeo-san."

"Hai, domo," Takeo says and heads for the bar.

Realizing he can't act unless Ushijimi gives him orders, which seems unlikely, Takeo can do nothing except observe. After two minutes, he sees his general make a gesture that can only mean to let Cho drink himself into oblivion. Takeo nods, but decides to continue to hang in the vicinity.

"Poker, anyone?" a tipsy adjutant shouts, and his shout is met with a boisterous chorus of approval from the officers who haven't passed out or aren't sprawled across the banquet tables in drunken stupor.

It causes Ushijimi to wince, but he says nothing. It's no secret about what he thinks about gambling, but he decides not to act on principle in this instance. Besides, it seems a good way to end the night. He nods his approval to the anxious wait staff, who scurry off to set up card tables in the bar area.

Aware of Ushijimi's feelings about gambling, but as an act of courtesy Admiral Ota asks him if he wishes to join them at their table, and isn't surprised when he declines.

"How about you, Colonel Harata?" Ota invites.

The colonel's face betrays his indecision. He wants to play, but he shakes his head. Even though fond of the game, he's come to realize he's no good at it. His problem is that he bets heavily and loses heavily. Fortunately he comes from a wealthy family, so his gambling losses aren't as bothersome as his in- jured ego. And yet… "Thank you, but no," he finally says.

"Come on, Colonel," Ota urges.

"I promised my wife I'd quit," Harata gives his excuse.

"You'd never make an artillery man," chides General Wada.

"Just this one time?" Ota pleads.

"Table stakes?" Harata asks.

"If you insist," Ota agrees.

"Okay, count me in," Harata concedes, and the three head toward the bar area where General Fujioka has already claimed one of the tables.

"Count me in," slurs General Cho, miffed that he hasn't been invited.

"Really, Isamu," Ota says. "Are you sure you can still see the cards?"

"I can see fine, sailor boy," Cho counters with slurred words.

"Maybe you'd better not, Isamu," Wada suggests in a soft voice.

"I said I was in!"

Takeo moves forward and tries to defuse the growing tension. "Please, General Cho, let's not make a scene. Ushijimi-chan is already upset."

"Keep out of this, jochu-san," Cho bellows. "Leave me alone or I'll slap the shit out of you, pretty boy!"

"I changed my mind," Harata says.

"What's the matter, Colonel Asshole? Chickenshit?" Cho says, shuffling forward to stand nose-to-nose with Harata.

Harata makes an attempt to spin away, but Cho grabs his arm and spins him around to face him once more. The colonel feels hot blood rush to his face.

"Cho-san!" Ushijimi shouts, moving forward to confront his drunken chief of staff. At the same time he glances at Takeo with a look that can only mean he's to stay out of these goings on.

Cho hesitates, and suddenly decides to pretend he hasn't heard. When Harata again tries to turn away, Cho spins him around once more and slaps his face. The other officers now back away.

"What's the matter, coward?" Cho challenges. "Are you afraid to play cards with a real man?"

"I'm not afraid of any man!" Harata shouts in a fit of temper.

"No?" Cho says with a snicker.

"No!" Harata responds.

"Then why not a little kendo match?"

"Why not!"

Ushijimi's anger is without bounds. What he's specifically forbidden is being disobeyed—by both officers. Cho might be the instigator, but Harata is complicit. Mitsuru takes only seconds before taking command of the situation. Nodding to Takeo to join him, he waits until the major stands beside him before he continues speaking.

"Kendo's a great sport, Kuroki-san. Did you participate?" Ushijimi asks in a start of a sham conversation.

"Hai, domo," Takeo responds. "I was champion at Zama."

"I thought so," Ushijimi says in controlled calmness. "I'm sure you'd appreciate witnessing a good kendo match, wouldn't you?"

Not waiting for Takeo to respond, he asks, "Can you arrange to furnish equipment for these two opponents?"

"Hai, domo."

Ushijimi now turns to the assembly of hushed officers and states, "It's settled. In the morning, General Cho and Colonel Harata will have a go at one another while Major Kuroki and I officiate. I'll be the judge."

A chorus of unintelligible mutterings come from the officers, but they hush when Ushijimi faces them and explains, "I'm sorry, my friends, that you will miss this contest. Remind me, please, to relate to you the results."

Turning to face the duelists, he declares, "Kuroki-san will furnish you equipment. Your bout will take place behind my quarters at zero-six-hundred hours! Be there!"

Neither Cho nor Harata indicates they've heard Ushijimi, but they have. What they do is continue to stare one another down, making intimidating snorts, even while they're aware that their commanding officer is striding angrily from the room.

Takeo hesitates not an instant before taking off, trying to catch up but is unable as he follows Ushijimi down the hallway and into the general's quarters.

"Can you believe those bakayaros?" Ushijimi shouts, digging for a cigarette. When struck, his match seems too intimidated to ignite, but afraid not to as it sputters into flame. After lighting his cigarette, Mitsuru flicks the prissy stick into an ashtray.

Sensing he's there only to listen, Kuroki says nothing.

Ushijimi continues. "You're correct, I suppose, if you think both of them are upholding their honor in this Bushido bullshit. What infuriates me is that at this moment both of them are penning words to the effect that if they are defeated, honor demands them to commit seppuku."

Takeo nods agreement.

"I warned them, Major, I warned them. I told them both that if they arrange for a duel I'd order both of them home in disgrace. I meant it."

"And now?" Takeo asks.

"They've got me in irons!" Ushijimi explodes and quickly calms. "The time is past when I can get replacements. The Americans may come at any time! I can no longer do what I said I would do! It's maddening!"

"I see," concurs Takeo.

"Do you?" Ushijimi says. "Meaning no disrespect, Takeo, maybe you do and maybe you don't. My problem is not keeping the fools from fighting, but keeping them from killing themselves. I need both minds."

"Sir, are you saying that you're going to let them fight?"

"Of course. In fact I'm rather looking forward to it. But the arrangements are not what they think. I have a plan, and you're going to play a role in it. Let me explain. Here's what I want you to do....."

6.

In the hush of the night, Takeo has errands to run. Forget sleep, forget everything except duty. Before dawn he has to locate kendo equipment—swords, uniforms, masks, and gloves—and deliver them to the combatants in their quarters, each man writing a letter he prays he'll never have to post.

Trying to overcome his anger over Cho's drunken rebuke, Takeo is in no mood to extend anything beyond minimum courtesy when he delivers the general's gear. He raps on the door and barges in without a word, then tosses the equipment at Cho's feet. Cho responds with a nod and a grunt and avoids eye contact.

Takeo's mood softens by the time he reaches Harata's quarters. As anticipated, he receives a gentlemanly greeting. The colonel is in a mood to talk.

"Ushijimi-chan must be angry with me?"

"Wouldn't you be, sir?"

"I completely understand how he must feel," Harata agrees.

"Then call it off, sir. You know he wants you to."

"I suppose he does."

"Then do it. Nobody will think the less of you."

"I can't, Takeo-san. You should know why it's not possible."

"No, I don't, sir. For Heaven's sake, why not? Is it a matter of pride?"

"One of honor," Harata defends. "If it were only pride, I'd do it without a qualm."

"There wouldn't be a question of honor or loss of face, sir. General Ushijimi will see to it, I'm sure."

"Did he ask you to say this, Major?"

"No."

"Then you can't say for certain, can you?"

"No, sir," Takeo answers. "But I know he'd make it so. He doesn't want you to fight. He needs you—both of you."

"Then he should be the one to tell us, shouldn't he?"

"He did, sir," Takeo says. "He told both of you."

"And General Cho disobeyed him."

"Cho was drunk, for God's sake!" Takeo states in growing agitation.

"But Cho was the one who started it."

"Did you have to join in?"

"No, I'm sorry to say."

"So neither of you has a leg to stand on, isn't that right?" Takeo reasons.

"That may be, Major. But the fact remains: Cho started it. And if Ushijimi-chan wants us to call it off, I'll have to hear it from the old man himself."

"Maybe you will, sir," Takeo suggests, ready to leave and head for his bed to grab a few winks of sleep before he has to get up.

"Takeo, before you go, may I ask a question?"

"Of course," Takeo answers, pausing on his way out the door.

"How is the staff taking this?"

"Talk is you can get two-to-one odds on your victory. As much as you want—up to twenty-thousand yen."

"That's horrible!" Harata says. "What kind of men bet on affairs of honor?"

"Soldiers, sir. We bet on anything. Rumor has it, the odds are three-to-five on the Americans winning the war."

Harata shakes his head, then ventures, "Wish me luck?"

"That I cannot do, sir. I hope you understand."

"I do," Harata responds and watches Takeo out the door with "See you in the morning, Major."

7.

Minutes before dawn—a silent time when the night dew has formed, scop owls and night herons have flown to roost, the smell of balsam is heavy in the morning mists, and the eastern sky is starting to hint crimson brilliance. The moon, three-quarters full and waxing, slips behind a cloud and when it emerges, dawn is breaking. It's a busy time for those involved in logistics for the coming duel.

Foregoing the luxury of sleep, Takeo finishes seeing to the preparations ordered by his daimyo. Jochu-sans have scalped the grass from a circular area suitable for kendo, but sentries have yet to posted to guard the dueling area.

In an ugly mood heightened by his lack of sleep, Takeo talks with the junior infantry officer commanding the unit ordered to post sentries and smells whiskey on the fool's breath. The lieutenant seems ready to give some sass, but a slap across his face ends that drama. As the orange tip of the sun broaches the horizon, Takeo checks again to make sure that sentries are at their posts, even if they're just pretending to be alert.

Shaking his shoulders and swallowing a yawn to fight sleepiness, he can't help but feel a rush of excitement at the anticipation of witnessing the big event soon to happen. He's not surprised when he sees Colonel Harata arrive on time, but he's a little suspicious about Cho showing up. Yet, suddenly here the general comes striding purposefully into view, all dressed up in his ill-fitting kendo outfit and showing no sign of hangover. Takeo's nose senses otherwise. The stench of Cho's sweat fouls the air. Takeo has to shake his head and admit, the man's capacity for alcohol is amazing.

Without speaking the opponents claim opposite sides in the circle of combat and begin their warm-up exercises, obviously improvised. Recalling his days at Zama, Takeo well understands how contrasting physiques will dictate their styles of fighting. The taller Harata, with his long arms, will be a fencer, while the stocky Cho has to be a mauler forcing himself inside to nullify Harata's definite reach advantage.

As his general's told him, Takeo takes his designated position one step behind and one step to the left of the canvas chair reserved for Ushijimi. Intent in observing the warm-up exercises, he all but misses Ushijimi's arrival. The man's just suddenly there.

"Both of you come to the center of the ring!" Ushijimi barks, and seems impatient when they choose not to run.

As they stand alongside each other at attention—Cho with his stocky build, his pouchy stomach he can no longer suck in, elbows in, knees tight, one hand clenched in a tight fist and the other holding his toy sword—and Harata with his sway-back posture, drooping shoulders, legs bowed with age, bony wrists without the sinews of youth, hair a shade of drawing-room gray—Takeo is struck with the thought that they're laughable, completely out of place in a combat arena.

Without fanfare, Ushijimi produces a scroll of rice paper, and after clearing his throat, begins to read from it. "As judge, I have written instructions to govern this contest. This is a sporting contest between Isamu Cho and Hiromichi Harata in the art of kendo. There's no glamour in this contest, but there is honor involved, and when honor is involved, consequences can be grave."

When he's seen both men blush their admission that he's onto their scheme, he continues. "You are bound by honor to abide by the rules of kendo, to fight honorably, and to give no quarter and expect none. You are bound under penalty of death by beheading to obey the judge. And obey, you had better! Disobey and you die like a common thief!"

At these words, Takeo takes one step forward, unsheathes his sword, and raises its blade into position before he steps back to resume his place. If Ushijimi gives the order, he's prepared to behead either man.

"As judge, I purify this arena with salt," Ushijimi states, tossing a handful of crystals upon the ground. "This is now a sacred place blessed by the Kami. You are both honorable men, and you will show your opponent the respect he deserves by bowing to him. You shall not engage in combat until I give the signal."

The duelists bow, first to Ushijimi and then to one another. They don helmets and face off, ready to fight.

"Engage!" Ushijimi shouts with high pitched shrill.

The opening moves by both men are graceful, skills remembered from years ago when they were young. For thirty or so furious seconds they parry and thrust, shout and grunt, and whack and defend like ancient samurai soldiers, demonstrating that at one time both must have been accomplished athletes.

After these early seconds, the skill level collapses. Sweat pours from their scalps and underarms to dampen the helmet pads and areas of the uniforms of both men, and the previous shouting is replaced with grunting, wheezing, and coughing from suddenly dry mouths. The clicking sounds from the collisions of their bamboo swords lessen noticeably in both frequency and intensity.

"Faster! Faster! Engage!" Ushijimi prods.

The combatants try their best to obey, and the pace of combat become again furious for no more than ten seconds, then again it slackens.

Suddenly Takeo feels surging pulse and he has to choke back a cry of excitement as he sees Cho slip and fall to one knee. Now he sees Harata's thrust finding empty air, allowing Cho to recover, rise to his feet, and resume his laborious stance, while Harata's sagging posture betrays his disappointment.

"Control your emotions, Major!" Ushijimi barks, and Takeo feels the blushing sting of being corrected.

The exhausted duelists are now crouching, holding their kendo swords at the ready, but making no indication they are prepared to either attack or defend.

"Engage, engage!" screams Ushijimi,. "I want action!"

Totally spent, both officers suck air and glance at one another, each unsure of how to reach down and find the strength to go on. But they find it, and both raise their swords and swing wildly. A sound of a weak click, the swords collide and fall side by side upon the ground, dropped by both combatants.

"Pick up your swords and fight!" Ushijimi shouts. "You two bakayaros had to have this thing. You had to go against my strict orders and make your stupid arrangement, so finish it! Fight, goddamn you, fight!"

Harata rises to one knee and Cho does likewise, but they're unable to rise any further. They glare at one another, not sure of what to do next.

"No?" Ushijimi shouts. "Major Kuroki-san, prepare to execute General Cho. And Colonel Harata will be next."

Takeo steps forward, stands next to Cho, and takes a power position to behead the whimpering general, who's now expecting oblivion.

"Enough of this farce," Ushijimi shouts. "Both of you listen carefully. I want your word of honor that you'll never disobey me again. Do I have it?"

Cho nods after slowly removing the helmet from his sweating head.

"Harata-san?"

"Hai," Harata is just able to mutter.

"Good! I declare this contest a draw!" Ushijimi says and starts walking way. But he stops, turns around, and adds, "Now you two bakayaros go to your quarters and cleanse yourself of your filth. Then be ready to resume your duties and help me take our army underground to await the Americans."

8.

Naha, 1945

Okinawans are tolerant people, but since the war began they see the French Catholic priest Pere Henri Marie Ferrand as a threat. He is, after-all, a foreigner, a gai-jin not to be trusted. In prior years they had come to know him as a kindly old man who seldom laughs, smiles a lot, and is so sure of himself that wherever he goes he's difficult to approach although he insists he's easy. Suspicions aside, they regard this holy man in charge of the Roman Catholic Mission on Okinawa as a most unusual man, even if he is getting along in years.

If pressed, Henri has to admit that age is taking its toll, but he refuses to fret, knowing that even if the vigor and sinews of youth diminish, he's blessed with enough strength to see to his mission while taking care of Kumiko, his teenaged ward. Henri's outlook is simply, so what if he is getting old? Isn't it true that while performance lessens, faith does not?

Yet it isn't by chance he's stopping to rest before he feels up to continuing on his way through Naha's residential streets and back alleys. One consolation is now he can watch the children playing in a nearby park. So Henri tells himself he isn't stopping to catch his breath, but to appreciate the frolicking young ones. The scene brings back memories of growing up in Carcassonne, that ancient city in the Languedoc, when everything the world has to offer was new, and each day was filled with the thrill of discovery. When did it stop being so?

In assessing his lot on Okinawa, he admits that times are bad. The reason is suspicion. The islanders now firmly believe they must avoid all gai-jins, even this harmless, friendly old priest clad in the frock of a Western holy man, one who's served them since 1931. Now, the tolerance he's worked fourteen years to gain is gone.

Stares and glares from children and elders make him uncomfortable, and the sight of anxious mothers scurrying to retrieve their children reinforces the feeling—another rebuff, another lament, another instance of unfounded fear. Henri understands. The reason is obvious. A little over a month ago, American planes appeared and bombed military installations near Naha. The bombers didn't do as much damage as the panic they caused. That soon changed. Two weeks later they came back, and this time they caused civilians to suffer. Worse, the American fleet has come to stay. Offshore, gray silhouettes of warships can be spotted hull down on the sea horizon any time of day.

Noticing afternoon shadows giving way to dusk, he realizes the need to get home before curfew. For several months, the authorities have heightened their surveillance of all gai-jins. After the air raids, the sirens were still sounding the all-clear when the military police hauled him in for questioning. He was in jail for two days before they let him go with a warning to stop doing whatever it is he's suspected of doing. Henri smiled, apologized, and promised to obey.

Home is the mission house in Naha, and from his first day he found it unlike any church or chapel he'd ever seen. The building began its existence as a dry goods store, and when that proved unprofitable, it became a warehouse. Then, when the Catholic Church began looking to establish a mission, the owners were willing to part with it for a reasonable price. Its transformation is in keeping with a frugal budget. The nave is open space without pews while the pulpit, altar, and chancel are also budget friendly. As a reminder of Christianity, a large wooden cross hangs by cast iron chains from the ceiling. Behind the chancel, two small rooms and a bare-bones kitchen serve as living quarters. Unlike the stale odor of the dust permeating the nave, a smell of fresh cleanliness is ever present in the living quarters.

Henri beats the curfew by minutes. As he steps inside the mission he hears Kumiko call his name in that assertive voice she's developed since she turned seventeen.

"Pere-san," he hears her demand. "It's almost curfew. Where have you been?"

"I was calling on a parishioner," he answers. "She lost her husband in the last air raid and needs prayer. Remind me, I must schedule a mass for him."

"Pere-san, you need to keep better track of time," she cautions. "Wherever you go, the police keep sharp eye on you. You give slight cause, they take you back to jail."

"I suppose," he sighs, finding her warning irksome, but he accepts it as another sign of the change he has to accept. By Okinawan standards, Kumiko is now mature, well into a period of life about which he hasn't the slightest experience.

She was only a tag-along little girl of three when her mother Kanai, a live-in housekeeper to Pere Fontaine, was finding it difficult to accept the new arrangements forced upon her and her child when this new priest arrives to replace Pere Fontaine, who's soon to retire and return to France. But she eventually accepts her new role of serving Pere Ferrand, who's here to stay.

As the mother explained, Kumiko's father was a fisherman from the village of Unten in the north, and he'd been lost at sea during a storm. Kumiko's grandparents are farmers near Chinen in the south of Okinawa, but they no longer acknowledge being related because of Kanai's conversion to the gai-jin religion. And when Kanai got sick and died three weeks after Pere Fontaine left, they made it clear they didn't want to have anything to do with raising her illegitimate child. Henri was beside himself with questions, but he ended up haggling with the authorities until they give permission for him to adopt her. From then on, he's been Kumiko's official guardian.

The next ten years were happy times for the unlikely pair, with Kumiko causing few problems, and certainly none compared to the joy she brought. Things got hectic when estrous arrived. He realized he could mess up and confuse the girl, so he hit on the idea of letting her schoolteacher handle the situation. She told him he'd have to prepare himself to get to know his ward all over again. Despite his doubts, he ended up thinking he'd done a pretty good job—but in no way is he prepared for her new attitude.

For sure Kumiko's living the life unique. She speaks two languages, lives with a gai-jin guardian, and worships his God. The only thing is, she's Okinawan and longs to be accepted by her long lost family. As puberty enhances her beauty, her attitude worsens, and Henri doesn't understand why. He keeps muddling through, but the questions—oh yes, there are the questions!

"Pere-san, c'est vous plait, what you know about Americans?" he hears her ask.

"Not much, cheri. I do know they're a Christian nation with good ties to the Catholic Church. That's about all."

"You think they cannibals?"

"Heavens, no, child," he declares. "America is a civilized country. Where did you hear such stories?"

"People say it. People say government claim their soldiers rape, kill, and destroy. Say they cannibals and eat children."

"Posh!" he says, "Stories like these are government propaganda."

"You sure?'

"Sans aucun doute."

Kumiko cocks a suspecting eye, although he's never lied to her before, and he seems to be sure of what he was saying. Still…?

"I can understand why you might be skeptical, Kumiko," he says. "If they're civilized, why would they bomb peaceful Okinawans?"

"Yes," she agrees. "Why?"

"It's hard to explain," he continues. "We're at war, and in war countries do horrible things to each. War is insane savagery."

"Nippon soldiers savage too?"

"I suppose," he answers. "But it's not wise to say it. I've lived too long under Japanese rule not to know they'd lock me up and throw away the key. And you too."

She nods her head in agreement, then turns to start out the door. She hesitates, then stops. There's something else on her mind.

"Pere-san," she asks. "Have you ever been in war?"

Like many other questions, this one takes Henri by surprise, and he's silent for long minutes while he ponders how to answer.

War? He thinks. *Yes, I've known it.* During his student days in Carcassonne's Jesuit Seminary of St. Nazaire, he interrupted his studies to volunteer as a military nurse in the Great World War. He drove an ambulance on the Western Front and experienced the fighting. The memories will last forever. He is almost in shock the first time he was in an artillery barrage. It was all he could do to pray with the wounded and hold their hands while they're dying. And he had personal tragedy—one brother killed in the trench fighting and another brother gassed and wounded. Finally, after that blessed Armistice Day in November of 1918, he returned to his studies. In 1926 he was ordained a priest in the Society of Jesus. Three years later, he volunteered to come to Asia as a missionary. On Okinawa, he discovered his purpose in life. Now it's threatened by invasion. With tears streaking his cheeks, he sees Kumiko still waiting for his answer. "Yes," he admits, "I have seen war."

"Would you tell me about it, Pere-san?"

"No," he whispers. "It's too painful."

Miffed at hearing a negative answer, she spins around and heads for the door.

"Where are you going?"

"Out," she snaps.

"Remember the curfew."

"The police don't bother me."

"Yukichi-san?" he explores, wanting to know if his suspicions about her and the young man she's been seeing are correct.

"Maybe," she admits, not willing to share the truth that she hasn't seen Yukichi since the day the planes sank the dredger he works on. But she speaks not a word as she goes out the door, closing it gently behind her.

She goes straightway to the waterfront and spots Yukichi sitting on one of the huge stones in the rip-rap area along the shoreline.

"I had an idea you'd be here," she says in greeting.

"I heard you coming. I recognize your footfall, you know," he answers.

"I haven't heard yours lately," she protests.

"I've been upset. They sank my dredger."

"Your dredger? Yukichi, you didn't even work on board the thing. The Japanese hold all the good positions. All you do is work on the pipeline crew—with the rest of the Okinawans."

"I'm working my way up."

"Fat chance!"

"It's no longer an issue," he says. "The dredger is gone, and so is my job."

"You can get other work," she says, trying to console the man who's big in her plans for the future. She loves Pere-san with her every fiber, but growing up without a family is painful. She wants one, and sweet and loving as he is, Pere-san can't give her that. She's determined to marry Yukichi and start a family of her own.

"So you missed me?" he asks.

"No," she lies.

"You did too."

"Maybe a skoshi," she admits, smiling.

"How much?" he asks, reaching for her breasts.

"Not that much," she states and pulls away.

"I suppose we're going to have the same old argument."

"I've told you a thousand times, Yukichi, not until we're married!"

"It's that religion your gai-jin guardian taught you," he grumbles. "That damned priest hates me, you know."

"Pere-son does not hate you! You make me mad."

"He's the reason you won't make love with me," he says. "It's not natural. You say you want us to get married, but you won't make love with me."

"No," she shouts. "It's immoral!"

"There! You get that from him."

"He's my guardian, for heavens sake," she says. "You forget I'm Catholic too. I was raised that way."

"As I said, the same old argument."

"You'll get a virgin on our wedding night," she says. "That's the way it's going to be. Can't you wait?"

They mope in silence until Yukichi says, "I enlisted in the Boetai today."

"You what?"

"Enlisted."

"That's so stupid!" she erupts and hits at him in tearful reaction.

"Calm down, Kumiko," he says. "It's logical; they were going to conscript me anyhow. They already spoke with my father."

"But you could have waited," she protests, feeling her world come apart.

"No," he says. "They're conscripting all young men. Some are as young as fourteen. I had no choice."

Kumiko grows silent for a spell, before falling into his embrace and asks "When are you leaving?"

"They're mustering us in the morning six days from now," he explains, "Our unit is marching north to Ie Shima—"

"I know where the island is," she interrupts.

"…where we're going to be trained to defend against the Americans."

"You'll be killed," she says, unable to stop her sudden flow of tears.

"Maybe—it's a possibility."

Kumiko lays back, takes Yukichi's hand in hers, and guides it to her breast. "Kiss me," she says.

9.

Six nervous days later, in the early morning of the day following Lunar New Year, Kumiko's period comes. She feels relief, although the realization she isn't pregnant with Yukichi's baby is bittersweet. It's also the day the Boetai are mustering for the march north to Ie Shima.

When the cold gray dawn of the morning breaks, a crowd has already formed in the marshaling area. Many of the young guardsmen have said their farewells at home, but many more are escorted to the area by their families, and everyone is milling around in clusters of twos or threes or fours, trying to act unemotional, brave, and patriotic. It's now when those who said their farewells at home begin to feel awkward and maybe a little unloved; Yukichi is among them, now regretting his false bravado of ordering Kumiko not to come and see him off.

Now the sight of her is suddenly overwhelming his vision. Without a word, he grabs her, pulls her into his embrace, and begins kissing the breath from her.

"You're late," he jokes, pulling away from the kiss.

"Oh, you!" she answers. "Did you really expect that I wouldn't be here?"

"I had my hopes," he admits.

The realization that their show of emotion has caught the attention of nearby Okinawans, who stop talking to gawk at this blatant lack of propriety, prompts the embarrassed lovers to step backwards and blush. When the gawkers seem satisfied that decorum has been restored, conversation resumes.

"Here," she says as she produces an irregularly shaped package covered with heavy cloth bound by stout rags.

"Let me see," he says, and begins fumbling with the rag knots.

"Don't open it now,' she instructs. "These are things I thought you might need."

"I insist," he says with a laugh. "You know how I adore surprises.'

"You're silly," she giggles, pleased with his insistence. "I know you, you know. I was certain you might overlook the basics. It's a little bag of rice along with a metal plate, a bowl and a spoon."

"You're right again," he confesses. "I do need these things, and I did forget."

"Pere-san wants me to say sayonara for him and to tell you he'll be praying for your safety."

Yukichi grunts, and after a pause mumbles "Tell him I said arrigato."

"I'll pray too," she says, feeling her vision blur from sudden tears she's told herself she wouldn't let happen.

"I know you will," he acknowledges, fighting to keep his own eyes clear.

A Japanese corporal in full field uniform with backpack suddenly starts blowing a whistle and shouting for the guardsmen to fall into ranks. The clusters of people begin to disband, mothers and sweethearts weeping softly and fathers fighting back manly tears. Japanese soldiers, previously unnoticed by the crowd, appear with rifles at the horizontal and begin to herd the civilians away from the marshaling area.

Kumiko hears herself mutter words that come out unintel-ligible, and she throws her arms around Yukichi and closes her eyes during their kiss. When she opens them, he is gone. She does not go to the mission chapel to pray as she had planned, but goes instead to the rip-rap boulder where she weeps until she can weep no more.

When she returns to the mission house, she goes to her guardian's room and finds him behind several reference books open on his desk as he writes.

"Pere-san," she begins. "What are you writing?"

"My sermon for Easter Mass," he answers, a tinge of an-noyance in his voice.

"That's what I want to talk with you about."

"Oh? How so?"

"While I was seeing Yukichi off, I heard people talking," she says.

"And? How does that affect my sermon?"

"People are leaving."

"So?"

"We should leave and go north like other people."

"North?" he stammers. "Why should we go north?"

"Pere-san," she says in a huff. "Open your eyes. The Japa-nese soldiers are all over the south. They've been building forts everywhere. That means they'll be fighting in the south. The north will be the only safe place."

Henri mulls it over and states "I agree. When we leave, we'll go north."

"We should leave now."

"We'll leave after Easter Mass," he insists.

"No!" she argues. "There will be fighting by Easter."

"Nonsense," he says. "I have told you the Americans are a Christian nation and will not desecrate Easter."

"I think you're wrong, Pere-san!"

"I have insight and experience you don't have," he explains. "Believe in what I say."

"And if you're wrong, and the Americans invade by Easter, we won't be able to go north," she states.

"And why wouldn't we be able to go north?"

"Because the Americans will invade at the peninsula beaches of Ishikawa."

"Says who?"

"The people," she answers. "I heard them say the invasion will be at Ishikawa."

"Those are rumors."

"I think maybe the rumors are correct."

"Which means you think I'm wrong and they're right," he argues.

"Yes, Pere-san, I do," she says as she turns to leave, but she turns back to tell him as she closes the door, "I'm afraid your insight and experience maybe get us killed."

10.

On the road to Ie Shima, 1945

If Yukichi Muragaki had any inkling about Japanese plans for defending Ie Shima, he wouldn't have enlisted, but fled as fast as he could for the wilds of northern Okinawa. What he doesn't know is that the Japanese consider the entire force on Ie Shima expendable. This strategy is based on Ushijimi's acknowledging that the Americans can capture the entire north whenever they want.

Two hours after the start of the Boetai's three days march to the north, the cool overcast of morning gives way to hot, sticky weather. Plodding along the dusty roads in ranks of four abreast, the ragged column's length stretches for a kilometer, and armed Japanese soldiers walk at irregular intervals alongside to maintain order. A single military truck follows to provide logistic support for the soldiers.

Still smarting from being told the Japanese have no intention of issuing rifles and ammunition to the Boetai, Yukichi's disappointment turns to grief when he finds out that in addition to carrying a blanket roll, each man has to lug a crate of ammunition. To make matters worse, the crates are not only heavy, but also made of the sort of splintery wood that makes carrying them awkward. Hardened by working long hours on the dredger pipeline crew, Yukichi is up to the task, but before they've gone ten kilometers many guardsmen are struggling to keep up.

Yukichi's experience with Jap taskmasters has taught him two things. Don't complain and don't sass. He cautions guardsmen within earshot they'd better do likewise or they'll come to grief. The wise heed the warning, but some don't and learn the hard way. An exhausted guardsman two rows behind him drops out to rest, and Jap soldiers ridicule, kick, and beat him until he rises, picks up his crate, and rejoins the column.

As the march continues kilometer after kilometer after kilometer, Yukichi ponders over something he hadn't thought through: Does he really hate anybody, even the Americans, enough to kill? Not for a moment has he ever believed Jap propaganda, but he's seen enough destruction from enemy air raids to know the Americans have to be stopped. Haven't they killed hundreds of innocent civilians for no reason? Didn't they sink his dredger? Does he think for a moment they won't kill him if they get the chance? And isn't it his duty to protect his homeland from the Americans from destroying it?

Obviously, the answer is yes, he does hate enough to kill. In the coming battle he might killed, but not before he settles the score. Oh, he'll fight so hard Kumiko will be proud! His parents, too. After the war they'll come to Ie Shima and stand before his tomb. Survivors of the great battle will tell stories about his bravery and of the many wounds he suffered before falling. They'll describe how in his fury he hurled grenade after grenade to take out three—no, it was four—tanks all by himself, and how his blazing guns kill a dozen—or was it two?—enemy soldiers before the rest run away rather than face him. When the island is at last secure, only then does he permit himself to lie down in a shady nook where he can bandage his bleeding wounds. Soon a colonel comes to kneel beside him and say, "My son, your valor has saved the island and the lives of your comrades. Well done, good and valiant soldier. Okinawans will never forget the legend of Yukichi Muragaki, mighty Boetai warrior" Now the colonel takes one of his own medals—the highest one—from his uniform and places it on the hero's bloody tunic. The colonel stands and salutes before taking reverent departure. As life's blood slowly oozes from his body, a shroud descends to bring gentle darkness. Now Kumiko comes to stand before his tomb (It's beside a shrine the government erects). As she softly weeps, his spirit comforts her, although she can't see or hear him. A gentle breeze springs up to balm her face and let her know his spirit is there, and she smiles, keeping faith with his memory. Oh, how beautiful his death!

A stumble and near fall wrenches him from reverie. Realizing he's probably made a damn fool of himself, he pays the price by suffering painful splinters in the palm of his hand when he all but drops his crate. Damn! Awkward and clumsy and stupid, he chastises himself and feels the heat of blood rising in his neck. Out of the corner of his eye, he catches sight of the man marching alongside flashing the hint of a silly little grin, meaning he finds it funny.

"Mind your own business!" Yukichi snaps, and finds satisfaction in seeing the man's grin run away before he shifts his crate to the other shoulder to hide his face.

In another second, Yukichi feels his face flush. The man's done nothing wrong. What matter the smile at his misstep? At this instant the man stumbles and almost falls and would have if Yukichi's hand doesn't reach out and steady him.

"Arrigato gozai masu," the man mumbles as he makes direct eye contact and beams a smile of gratitude.

"Dou itashi mashite," Yukichi replies, returning the smile, and quickly adds "Sumi masen—my bad manners."

"I never gave it a thought," the man says.

"I'm really not like that," Yukichi explains. "I don't know what got into me."

"Now it's my turn to say dou itashi mashite," the man laughs.

With a furtive glance, Yukichi takes stock of him and likes what he sees. The young man wears an easy smile with friendliness in his handsome face atop a muscular neck and a large, healthy body. He's tall—unusually so for an Okinawan. Yukichi has to admit he's never worked alongside anybody, young or old, the equal of this tall, muscular stranger. Yukichi has the quick thought he's happy Kumiko hasn't met the likes of this handsome young stranger.

"I'm Yukichi Muragaki from Naha, and I'm a dred-german—or at least I was before American planes sank my dredger," Yukichi says.

"Kozen Kokuba is proud to meet you," the big man comes back at him. "I'd bow in respect, but there's this damned crate prevents me."

Yukichi chokes back a laugh. "Yes, they seem to have that affect."

To preserve strength, even at the cost of friendliness, the two resume silence as the long column trudges on. The hours drag by. The Jap soldiers are not willing to allow the guardsmen to stop for rest. Each weary man digs deep down for strength to trudge on.

It's well after dark when the Japanese finally halt the march and instruct the guardsmen to set up bivouac in an open field beside the road. Yukichi says nothing, but he's pleased when Kozen tosses his blanket roll near his.

"I'm pooped," Yukichi mutters, dropping to his knees. He has presence of mind to hide Kumiko's package beneath the folds of his blanket.

"Me, too," Kozen agrees, spreading his blanket.

"Has this been anything like you expected?" Yukichi asks.

"To tell the truth, I didn't know what to expect," Kozen responds. "Did you?"

"No idea at all."

"Let's get some kindling and lay a fire. I'm hungry," Kozen declares, taking off to lay claim. Other guardsmen are doing the same.

"We can also have tea. I brought a teapot," Yukichi adds, getting to his feet.

Their search is timely. They find a trove of dead tree branches and carry them back to where they'd left their belongings.

"Damn!" Kozen curses.

"What's wrong?"

"One of our so-called honorable fellows stole my rations," he says and groans.

"Assholes! You can't get away from them," Yukichi declares, glad he's hidden his beneath the blanket.

"I guess I'm lucky they didn't take my tripod and kettle, but they left me with nothing to eat," Kozen says,. "Not a damned thing."

"We'll share," Yukichi chimes in.

"That's noble, but it's not right," Kozen objects, unsure of what he's going to do.

"You have to eat, Kozen. We'll share. And let's hear no more about it."

"If you insist, but only if you're sure you have enough," Kozen states. "Arrigato gozai masu—again!"

"We have what we have and no more, so don't argue. And dou itashi mashtie—again," Yukichi responds.

Kozen bows low and declares, "I've never before made such a good friend so quickly, Yukichi-san. I'm forever in your debt."

Yukichi smiles and returns Kozen's bow, thinking for a brief moment he's almost glad somebody stole Kozen's rations.

When the fire's going good and the rice is boiling, they sip tea and are ready for conversation. Yukichi begins by telling Kozen about life on the pipeline crew and as he talks, he's pleased to find his new friend's a good listener, quiet and patient and interrupting only when he wants an explanation about a point or two he doesn't understand. When it's Kozen's turn to talk, he proves to be a good storyteller as well as a listener. On both counts he earns respect for his social skills.

Kozen describes himself as a farm boy living at home on the family farm in the south. He calls it a life uncomplicated, but secure. They raise sweet potatoes and make a good living until three years ago when the military government began confiscating the crop to make alcohol. They promise the farmers will receive equal value in rice and other foodstuffs, only the exchange system turns out to be complicated, unfair and fraught with larceny. The farmers lose and can't complain.

Kozen explains his large size is a family mystery. Of course, his mother is beyond reproach, so his father just accepts it when that he grows to stand a head taller than any of his four older brothers. All five of them enlist together because they want to stay together, but it doesn't turn out that way. While his brothers are assigned to Boetai units in the south, he's singled out for assignment to the Ie Shima contingent. He doesn't mind going to Ie Shima, but he's very disappointed to be separated from his brothers.

"I don't make friends easily," he confesses. "Not like you do. You're different somehow—the sort that's easy to get to know."

After their scant meal, just enough to knock the edge off of their appetites, they face off in silence across the decaying fire, and when it dies to glowing embers with barely enough red-light power to see by, Kozen excuses himself, curls up on his blanket and sleeps.

Yukichi doesn't drift off immediately, but lets his reverie return to the last time he sat with his grandfather to watch a summer moonrise in August when the moon is full and very orange. It turns out to be grandfather's last August moon in his long life, and this sweet memory brings sleep.

Stiff and sore to a man, the Boetai are rousted out by the Jap soldiers at dawn, and there's barely time enough to restart the fire, heat water for tea, and search out a private place to do their morning toilet before the Japs begin shouting for them to fall in for muster. All too soon the column is again trudging north, and after what seems like an eternity, they approach the fishing village of Nago, where the road bends westerly onto the Mobotu Peninsula. They bivouac soon after the village fades from sight. Still sharing Yukichi's rations, both bed down and fall asleep with unsatisfied appetites.

As on the previous morning, they're rousted out at dawn to resume the march. As the sun gets higher, many of the weaker guardsmen are in distress and have to fall out of ranks. The Jap soldiers round them up and form them into a stragglers unit, loading the abandoned crates onto the truck following the formation. Jap guards hold the stragglers in contempt and treat them accordingly.

When the sun's at its zenith, a formation of enemy planes appears, and the guardsmen break for cover. Yukichi and Kozen dive headfirst into a drainage ditch beside the roadway and find themselves facedown on matted of pine needles as they wait fearfully for the planes to attack. When they dare to raise their heads, they're relieved to see the airplanes holding formation and continuing to fly south.

On the road again, the Boetai continue until late after-noon when they stagger into the town of Bise on the tip of Mobotu Peninsula. Here they're told to fall out and surrender their crates to workers who load them onto motor launches moored at a jetty. Rid of their crates, they are dismissed and fall exhausted upon a grassy knoll and rest until they bivouac for the night. In the morning the Jap soldiers herd them into lots of fifty and tell them stand fast until they're called away to board a boat for the short voyage to Ie Shima.

Although the sea is calm, Kozen gets seasick before the boat clears the breakwater and is soon suffering from dry heaves. Yukichi manages to keep a straight face and offer sympathy. When the voyage is over, Kozen tells Yukichi, "I guess I'm not a sailor. Arrigato for not laughing, but I saw you smile."

When the Boetai fall into formation, they are fed by the Japanese and given the rest of the day off to relax and bivouac near the base of Iegusugu Yama, the island's extinct volcano. The next morning, in unusual display of laxity, the Japanese do not hold revile, but let the guardsmen sleep till noon when they're given a light lunch of fish broth. Then they assemble for assignment to work details.

Yukichi and Kozen are assigned to the same detail, forty guardsmen led by a Jap soldier. They're told they'll be working for the support group of the Ie airbase. The Jap soldier in charge is a private, a nondescript little man who seems as much out of place as any of his laborers. In friendly tones he talks a bit too much about himself, telling them how he used to own a small vegetable farm near Beppu in Kyushu. He admits he hates army life and was conscripted, probably to appease the desire of a petty bureaucrat who'd taken a shine to his wife. He says he's now divorced.

When they muster next morning, they find that their little private is no longer in charge, replaced by a corporal who is bigger, louder, and easy to hate. He leads the detail to a large pile of green bamboo and tells them to start building dummy airplanes. "They draw fire from the enemy," he tells them. They grab bamboo and get to work, and by nightfall the bamboo's used up. The next morning there's another pile of bamboo and soon the number of dummy planes grows steadily.

Just before noon sirens wail. A few guardsmen stand and look skyward, but most take a cue from the corporal and start running. Yukichi doesn't wait for Kozen and follows the corporal until he spots a series of slit trenches. He reaches them just as the planes begin their attack, and like the corporal he dives headfirst into the first one he sees, vaguely aware of the roaring planes making pass after pass and shooting at the parked Japanese aircraft. He lands facedown, eyes closed, petrified with fear, cowering in the volcanic grit at the bottom of the trench. He clamps his hands over his ears in a vain attempt to silence the sound of bombs exploding nearby, and abruptly an earth tremor shakes loose a slice of the trench wall. It peals away and drops onto his quivering body, making him scream, tense, and piss his pants.

The terror continues for time unrestrained, and then suddenly there is wonderful silence. He continues to hold his prone position before summoning the courage to stand and emerge from the trench. He looks about. A roaring oil fire is consuming the skeleton of a hangar, as turbulent spheres of fire and rolling black smoke thrust straight up into the sky. Secondary explosions of gasoline drums punctuate the rhythm of the hangar fire. He sees a Japanese damage control party charging the fire, but they give up and let it burn. Parked planes and bamboo dummies are in shambles, and both runways have been cratered. A damage control team advances toward an unexploded bomb, but as they close in, the bomb explodes and they are suddenly no more.

Awareness of senses gradually returns, and Yukichi has the presence of mind to have concern for Kozen. He glances around—and now Kozen appears. The two giggle at the joy of being alive, and their giggles turn to laughter when each discovers the other's piss strains. "Follow me!" Yukichi shouts and leads Kozen to the beach where they laugh and splash in the surf and remove the embarrassing evidence.

11.

Ie Shima

After the first air raid, the Americans don't bother attacking Ie Shima for a while, so the Japanese can finally get around to teaching the Boetai to shoot. The government has a rule against Okinawans owning guns, so along with the others neither Yukichi nor Kozen ever handled a rifle.

The first thing they learn is they won't be issued rifles, although each man is given two bullets and told he's responsible for them. With bullets in hand, the next thing they hear is a Jap officer explaining how the drill will consist of two army infantrymen showing each man how to shoot. They'll instruct them how to load, aim, and fire his weapon. Then when the soldier considers that the man has the hang of it, he'll tell him to load the rifle and shoot twice at the target.

The instructors assigned to Yukichi's squad couldn't be more opposite. One is a sergeant, a non-sweating, sweet-smelling huge man with the look of a sumo apprentice, wrestler, while the other is a smallish spit of a corporal with darting eyes that seem to shine like a starry black sky. The sergeant does all the talking; his words are terse, spoken with flawless grammar drawn from a rich vocabulary. Both Yukichi and Kozen get the feeling they wish these two had been assigned to another squad.

The sergeant's instructions are brief, confusing, and condescending. As he speaks, his soft hands toy incessantly with a riding crop, quick to deliver a sharp blow to the wrist of any man making a mistake. After each guardsman finishes firing his bullets, the sergeant dismisses him with a crack from his riding crop.

When Kozen steps forward for his turn, the sergeant's reaction is dramatic. His mood brightens, his voice becomes soft and vivacious, and his attitude bubbly. Yukichi is almost alarmed when he sees Kozen blush and gaze at the ground. He's obviously embarrassed about the sergeant's clear show of favoritism.

Even as Yukichi watches, he becomes aware of the corporal moving in to stand close behind him. Yukichi takes a deep breath and waits. "Your friend had better watch himself," he hears the corporal whisper.

"What?" Yukichi asks in undertone.

"The sergeant's cute."

"I don't understand."

"He's an abuser; he likes men," the corporal explains.

"That can't be!"

"Oh, no?" the corporal continues. "He's had his prick up the ass of half the men in our platoon."

Yukichi would like to delve further, but after giving his warning the corporal moves on. He's suddenly aware that the sergeant's previous mood is back, and so when his turn comes, he's almost relieved when he feels the pang in his wrist from the riding crop. When it's time to shoot, he jerks the trigger and misses the target with both shots.

After the drill, he catches up with Kozen and falls in alongside as they head for the bivouac area. Kozen is sullen and silent, and Yukichi doesn't press the point, satisfied to wait for his friend to get into the mood to speak. Breaking his silence, Kozen says, "Do you know what that fat sonnuvabitch whispered to me?"

"I can imagine," Yukichi answers. "The corporal warned me about him."

"It's not fair!" Kozen roars.

"Nothing is when the Japs are concerned."

"I must have been born under a bad star," Kozen complains.

"Evening meal is about ready. Let's go," Yukichi suggests, hoping to get Kozen's mind off of his problems.

"No, you go," he hears Kozen answer. "I'm going down to the beach and think."

"You've got to eat."

"I'm not hungry," Kozen says as he heads for the beach.

After evening meal Yukichi returns to their tent, hoping to find Kozen there. When he isn't, Yukichi sets off for the beach to look for him. The sea is calm, the moon is deep into its first quarter and already set, so there's only starlight and the fluorescence from the gentle surf to illuminate the scene. A light sea breeze mutes the sounds of the waves breaking on the shore and makes the air smell of seaweed and ocean creatures.

Kozen is nowhere to be found, but Yukichi seems to hear voices—faint, unintelligible sounds of words being spoken. What's plain is that the words are angry and demanding. He heads toward the source of the voices and lies down on a berm where he can make out silhouettes of soldiers against the light of the luminous surf.

Creeping forward to get a better look, he stops when he's close enough to see the men. There are four of them—one is Kozen, one is the sergeant, and the other two he's never seen before. Like the sergeant they have the size and hulk of sumos. The two wrestlers have tight hold of Kozen's arms and hold him erect while the sergeant speaks in demanding voice as Kozen protests and resists.

Unable to help his friend, Yukichi continues to watch. Abruptly the sergeant turns and walks farther down the beach with the two wrestlers dragging Kozen along, and the four of them are now out of earshot. In the next instant the sergeant starts hitting Kozen repeatedly in the stomach until Kozen goes limp and falls from the grasp of the wrestlers into the surf.

Furious at being unable to help, Yukichi's anger isn't enough to overcome his fear, and with disgust at himself he sneaks away until he's able to stand and run away. When he arrives at last to the bivouac area he charges into their tent, falls upon his bedroll and mutters to himself, "The dirty Jap bastards, those dirty Jap bastards!"

His rage isn't yet spent when he hears Kozen enter, but he keeps his eyes tightly shut and feigns sleep when his friend lies down and begins sobbing, until blessed sleep comes to comfort them both.

Far from being normal in any respect, the following day is taken up with instruction about how to use a bayonet. When the day is over, and he and Kozen have turned in for the night, he hears two men come to the edge of the tent and call softly for Kozen to come out. Yukichi again feigns sleep and doesn't dare move as he hears Kozen get up and join them. Only after they are gone does he allow tears to come.

12.

Okinawa, 1945

In the midnight hour before Easter Sunday, April 1, 1945 ships of the United States Navy are on the move in the East China Sea. Offshore from the sandy beaches south of the Ishikawa Peninsula, troop transport ships of the American Invasion Fleet silently steam in and drop anchor. Weather is ideal—cloudy with clearing skies, moderate seas, comfortable temperatures, and balmy breezes. At dawn the Americans Tenth Army will come ashore in force. Their beachhead at Hagushi will span eleven kilometers from flank to flank. They'll be surprised to find no Japanese resistance.

13.

Naha, Easter Sunday

As Easter dawns, American big guns open up on Naha. The first projectiles hit beyond the designated targets and explode in the neighborhood of the Catholic mission. Within an area of several city blocks, buildings erupt in explosions and begin to burn. The mission survives, but it's rocked, shaken, and damaged by bursting shrapnel.

Shaken from deep sleep from the explosions, Pere Ferrand instinctively yells out "Mon Hevene!" Memories of horrible days in the trenches come flooding back to renew mental recognition of the source of the sound and percussion. Pulling his wits together, he bolts out of bed while overcoming an impulse to crawl under it and hide.

When he's fully aware of what's happening, he accepts reality and is furious. The invasion is here. The Americans are invading. The heathens are desecrating Easter. Kumiko was right. Why didn't he listen? He grits his teeth, realizing too late the foolishness of his decision to overrule her.

"What a miserable creature am I," he shouts into the dark. There's an urge to kneel and pray, but he does not. Instead he begins fumbling aimlessly in the darkness while his mind fills with the thought he must do something, even if it's just getting dressed. He's standing in his indecisiveness when the door bursts open and Kumiko rushes across the room and throws her arms around his neck. It takes every bit of his soothing attention to quiet her, even as he hears her gasp and feels her maturing body tense at each of the continuing explosions, near or far. "Go dress, child, then meet me in the sanctuary," he instructs, trying to disarm his ward's panic. The sound of her shuffling away in the darkness is gratifying.

Still in his nightgown, he's now obsessed with the idea to go to the chancel and pray. Prayer will give him direction. He's in the chancel, kneeling in prayer at the altar when Kumiko enters, dressed and packed and ready to travel.

"Pere-san!" she erupts, more distressed than angry. Dropping her traveling pack she charges over and kneels beside him.

"Come, we go now," she commands.

Henri says nothing, just continues in prayer.

"Pere-san!"

"Yes, child," he answers in a whisper.

"We have to go now."

"Go? Go where?"

"To safety," she says. "It's not safe here any more."

"Where would that be?" he asks in calm voice. "Where could we possibly go that is safer than God's house?"

"Away," she screams. "Far away from the fighting."

"And where will you find it on this island?" he asks, keeping his eyes closed in his prayer vigil.

"South, north, anywhere but here. They can't be fighting everywhere at once," she screams, annoyed at her guardian's condescension.

"Can't they?"

"No," she shouts. "It's not possible. Open your eyes, Pere-san. You have to realize what's happening."

Even in the dark she can sees her guardian's eyes remain closed, and she's about to complain when a deafening explosion overwhelms their senses. A thunderous concussion follows and a choking cloud of dust, dirt, and grime engulfs the chancel even as pelting bits of flying rubble pepper the two of them. In the next second, the overhanging wooden cross is torn from its chains and comes crashing down with large chunks of the old building's earthen structure. For an instant they're both sure they've been killed.

Henri slowly gains presence of mind to extricate himself from the rubble. His first thought is Kumiko's safety and he reaches to clasp her arms now locked around his neck.

"Yes, my child," he says over her whimpering. "We will go. We will go away from the fighting. Where that it, I don't know. But God willing, we will find it."

Crimson firelight from a blazing adjacent building cast long shadows and provides enough crimson illumination for them to see the devastation of the mission. Kumiko calms, examines her guardian, sees blood spilling from a hairline cut along his left temple, and cries, "Pere-san, you're hurt."

"It's nothing," he says. "I'm not even aware of it."

"Not so! It's running into your eye. I have to dress it."

Extricating herself from the rubble, Kumiko runs to where she's dropped her backpack and rummages through it until she locates a small first-aid kit, from which she takes gauze, a bottle of mercurochrome, and a jar of petroleum jelly before returning to where her guardian is standing, looking at the fallen cross.

"Such a waste," he moans.

"Hold still," she orders and begins cleansing and dressing his wound, not satisfied until she's bandaged his temple with a knotted bandana to hold the gauze in place.

Over his protests, she orders him to go get dressed and pack whatever he needs to travel on foot. As he lumbers off, she repacks her backpack before making her way through the rubble to go out the door to wait.

She peers around. Everything is strange, not at all like the neighborhood she knew mere hours ago. The street is strewn with rubble, there are open spaces where there weren't any before, the air smells of burning wood and ancient mortar, and the atmosphere is filled with smoke and fine dust that seems constantly changing color in reflecting light from fires burning out of control. What isn't there are people; the streets are deserted. She catches sight of movement and stares until she can make out the forms of two men moving in her direction. Afraid at first they might be soldiers, she's relieved as they come nearer to see they're policemen. She hails them, and they walk in her direction. "What's happening?" she asks. "Is it the invasion?"

"Yes," one of the policemen replies.

"Can you tell me where they're coming ashore?"

"In the north," the policeman answers.

"Hagushi?"

"Looks like it," the policeman answers.

The response makes her stomach muscles tighten, and then she asks "We were planning to go north to Mobotu. Is this possible?"

"I wouldn't advise it," the policeman answers.

Kumiko notices that one policeman is doing all the talking and she wonders if it isn't because the other might be in a bit of distress. "Are you all right?" she asks.

"My friend here lost his entire family tonight," the first policeman explains. "I'm proud of him for wanting to continue doing his duty under these circumstances."

"I'm so very sorry," Kumiko says, reaching out to hold the man's hands.

"My two children were so beautiful and playful—like my wife," he blubbers, and then he looks at the other policeman with askance that they move on.

"We'd better go," the first policeman says. "I wouldn't go north, because the Americans are there in force. Their ships are all over the horizon. But wherever you go, leave now—immediately. They're shelling us from large ships, and planes are bombing and strafing the waterfront area. Fires are everywhere. Leave while you can. Sayonara."

She watches the two policemen trudge off, and then she turns to see what's delaying Pere-san. Leaving her backpack by the front door, she re-enters the building and groans at what she sees. He hasn't moved; he's still in his nightgown and stands there gazing around. The sight makes her grit her teeth as she steels her feelings.

"Pere-san!" she shouts, void of sentiment. "We have to go!"

"Patience, child. I'm not nearly ready to go—not nearly ready."

"There's no time, Pere-san. We have to go—now!"

"There are things I must do."

"Things? What things?"

"There are so many things I must pack."

"I packed most of your clothes yesterday," she explains. "All you have to do is finish dressing, add your razor and toothbrush to your pack, and then we leave."

"Clothes? Razor? Toothbrush?" he mumbles. "I need other things besides my clothes and toilet articles."

"What?"

"My vestments. I must take my vestments—my alb, my amise, and my Bible and my Missal—and my chalice. I just can't go rushing off and forget my mass articles."

"Oh, all right," she agrees with the thought that the silver chalice might have bartering value if it comes to that, and the white linen alb will make clothing or bandages if the need arises. As she waits with annoyance at the waste of precious minutes, she does her best to remain calm until Henri appears, now dressed in his grey robe and carrying two packs.

"I'm ready—I think," he mumbles.

"One last thing," she says.

"What?"

"Water, Pere-san," she explains, handing one of a pair of canteens she'd made from stoneware jugs suspended from knotted macramé.

Henri takes a final look at the mission's wrecked interior before heading for the door, and Kumiko follows herding him along. Daylight is beginning to invade the night, but smoke and the smell of devastation hang heavy in the air.

"We'll go north," he directs.

"South," she corrects.

"But I thought—" he starts to say.

"You thought wrong," she interrupts,. "The Americans are in Hagushi. A policeman told me. It's too late. We can only go south."

"Oh, dear," he mumbles, remembering her warning that the south is where the Japanese military built their defenses. Her unspoken meaning is clear. They've been trapped in the area sure to be the scene of the fighting. *Oh Lord,* he thinks. *Nothing is going right.*

The American bombardment now ceases, so their only threat comes from the fires and smoldering rubble from wrecked buildings. They start groping their way through the narrow streets leading south. Fires rage out of control with nobody fighting them, and the odor of burning flesh putrefies the air, so relief comes when they finally see high ground rising beyond the edge of the city. They feel exhaustion, and the day is just beginning.

Henri suddenly stops and looks around, struck with the thought he hears the faint sound of a bawling baby—and there it is again—and now he's certain. Dropping his packs and water jug, he raises the bandage to uncover both ears, and begins to turn his head from side to side, listening until he's sure of the direction of the source.

Sans doute, he tells himself. *These are cries of a baby*. Setting off in the supposed direction, he advances until he discovers a ragged, filthy infant sitting alone in the midst of a pile of rubble and charred timbers of what was once a house. The cries are weak, almost without the energy to continue. "Me voici. Allons, allons," he speaks, scooping the baby up into his arms.

"Pere-san! What are you doing?" Kumiko is suddenly shouting from the street.

"Saving this child," he says.

"Where are the parents?" Kumiko asks, knowing that giving in to him now would result in his taking in every waif they come across.

"Je ne voyons personne," he answers in his native French as he looks around.

"Qu'avez-vous dit?"

"Personne. I see no one—not even a corpse."

"Pere-san," she declares. "We can't care for the baby."

"We can't let her die!"

"It's not possible!"

"We must! In God's name, we must! This is a child of God and my responsibility," he asserts.

"And how do you intend to provide for your responsibility, you crazy old man?"

"I cannot and will not abandon this child," he announces, glaring at his ward and suddenly wondering what sort of a child has he raised?

Kumiko does not answer.

"…nor any child!" he concludes.

"And how do you intend to provide for them?"

"God will provide," he affirms. "He always does, always has and always will."

"Will He?"

"If you doubt this, if you doubt God's mercy for innocent children, if you do not believe that you can serve as His instrument to serve them, if you are so concerned about your own well-being that you are ready to abandon helpless infants, then go! Go on alone. I don't need you. In fact the last thing I need now is a rice-Christian," he declares.

To Kumiko, Henri's words are a slap across her face. Tears well in her eyes, and she hangs her head and weeps. "I'm sorry, Pere-san," she's finally able to gasp. "You're right and I'm wrong. Please, Pere-san, can you find it in your heart to forgive me?"

Henri stands comforting the infant while slowly letting the indignation die until he's able to say "Haven't I always?"

Kumiko's tears stop, and with a little laugh of embarrassment she runs the short distance to her guardian, takes the baby from him, and cradles it in her arms. "The baby's so dirty I can't tell if it's a boy or girl," she says. "Regardless, it needs water."

After giving the infant water Kumiko tears a strip from her blouse and uses it to cleanse the grime from the little body, until she exclaims, "She's a little girl, probably not yet a year old. We found her just in time."

The child has soiled herself, so the rest of Kumiko's blouse becomes a diaper. Fortunately the baby's little bottom shows no festering sores or scrapes. Kumiko hands the baby back to her guardian to hold while she digs into her backpack for another blouse, and after donning it takes the child back, handing into her backpack to Henri, who now has to lug it along with his other two packs and one water jug.

"We go now," she instructs.

They continue trudging south until they exit the city and melt into the exodus from Naha. With their agonizing pace with frequent stops for rest, it isn't long before they're again alone, out of sight from the other refuges.

About midmorning echoes from the distant explosion from Naha cease altogether. Continuing the slow trudge south with no thought of destination, they stop exhausted and watch April's first sunset until dusk invades the countryside. Kumiko chooses a plot of open ground beside the road as their campsite for the night. It's not a good campsite, but it will have to do because they lack the strength to go any further.

With unspoken agreement of assignments, Henri tends to the baby while Kumiko prepares a fire, bakes sweet potatoes, and heats water to thin honey. Henri surrenders his share of their meager ration to the famished baby, who cries for more, but Kumiko firmly shushes her. The baby quiets, fusses a bit and drifts off into sleep. This allows Kumiko to sleep. Undisturbed in the still of the night, Henri says his prayers and only then does he fall asleep, leaving the crickets to own the night.

Starlight is fleeting and everything's damp with dew when Henri and Kumiko awake to the cries of the baby. Both adults are vexed about hygiene not performed and are humiliated with the realization that it's not possible. Henri's headband came off during the night, but blood from the wound has crusted into an unfeeling scab. Over Kumiko's objection he decides to leave it bare.

The baby had soiled herself with loose stools during the night, so cleansing her becomes was a disgusting chore for Kumiko, who stares at her guardian until he nods permission to sacrifice his alb for swaddling clothes. Breakfast repeats last night's diet, and after they have finished eating and feeding the baby, Kumiko makes another decision about the use of Henri's alb.

"Pere-san," she says. "Before we take another step I am going to clean this child from top to bottom. And what's more, we are going to give her a name."

Henri's smile is agreement.

"All right," she says. "What's it to be?"

"That's up to you, I think."

"No," Kumiko objects. "Miserable soul that I am, I would have left her."

"Not for long, I think. You would have changed your mind."

"You believe that or just trying to spare my feelings?"

"I'm positive," he answers. "and what's more, you did. Child, we all need help from time to time."

Her eyes show reticent agreement as she winks her thanks at him, before turning away so he can't see the tears welling in her eyes.

"Well," Henri says. "Have you thought of a name?"

"I'm still thinking about it, Pere-san. Giving a child a name she will carry for the rest of her life is a great responsibility and deserves great thought, no?"

"If you say so."

Their happy mood carries over until they are once again on the road. Somehow they manage to reach the high country, where they see numerous large gan turtle-tombs built into the hillsides. Kumiko recalls hearing rumors about the Japanese turning gans into gun emplacements. Neither she nor Henri can see soldiers, but they sense themselves being watched from distant heights.

With no plan of escape, realization comes that they're at the mercy of wherever the road leads, and several kilometers bring them to an elevated plateau where the landscape flattens to reveal farmland, patchworks of small hectare plots. Mid-morning finds them trudging along this same dirt road.

Outside the farming settlement of Tera, the road forks, and they stop to rest before deciding which way to go. The sound of motors in the distance soon becomes a convoy of military trucks raising dust along the southeasterly fork, to the decision becomes clear; they'll take the other fork. A signpost points this way to the village of Iwa.

In an hour, they trudge with weary legs into Iwa, and immediately a village elder appears and tells them they can't stay. When asked why, the elder gives two reasons: First, Henri is a gai-jin, and this will make the Japanese soldiers angry if they find him here, and secondly Henri is not only a gai-jin, but also a Christian who'd anger Iwa's ancestral gods. Kumiko is ready to argue, but Henri forbids it with the simple explanation that they had asked for help and it has been denied. It's clear that they have no choice but to continue on.

They proceed through the village with the village elder escorting until they arrive at the outskirts where he stops and continues watching to make sure they don't stop. No more than fifty meters beyond the edge of town, they hear the elder shout, "Here, take some more of your Naha trash with you."

The elder turns and barks orders to a group of village women who now appear and forcibly push a young girl from their midst. The elder then points his finger at her to join Henri and Kumiko. The girl just stands there undecided until an old woman throws a clod of dirt at her. The child takes flight and runs down the road toward Henri and Kumiko, but stops just short. On the verge of tears, she stares them down and stands her ground in defiance to strange circumstance.

"What's this?" Kumiko demands, instantly regretting her words.

"Hush!" Henri snaps at Kumiko and turns to say to the girl, "Come her, cheri."

The girl continues to stand and stare.

"Don't be afraid. We won't hurt you," Henri says, dropping his load and stoops to beckon with open arms. Still, the girl refuses to come.

"Quickly now!" Kumiko barks. "Do as Pere-san says."

Terrified, the child leaps forward and charges into Henri's waiting embrace. Henri feels her forehead press tightly against his chest. Tears streak down her dirty face, and she sobs while Henri strokes her hair until he feels the fear go out of her.

"Who are you? Where did you come from? How did you get here? Where is your family?" Kumiko asks in gentle voice in her rush of questions, even as she hears a bubbling grunt coming from the baby in her arms as the infant reaches out for the girl in Henri's embrace.

The girl breaks free and looks at the baby with the surprised light of recognition in her eyes. The girl and the baby stare at one another in silent communication. "I know her," the girl says, turning her head to look directly into Henri's eyes.

"From where, cheri?" Henri asks.

"You're a gai-jin?" the girl says.

"He's a priest, a man of God," Kumiko states defensively.

"Do you mean like those men at Nami-No-Ue-Gu near my home?"

Knowing that particular area of Naha well, Henri realizes she's referring to a Buddhist Temple on a hill near the Tomari International Cemetery where all the westerners are buried. Pere Adnet, the first Roman Catholic missionary on Okinawa, has rested there for a hundred years.

"No, cheri," Henri says. "I'm a Christian priest, not Buddhist."

"I'm a Buddhist, me and my grandmother," the girl explains. "Next week it's going to be Hanna-Matsuri, grandmother says, and we're going to the temple, she says."

"That's nice," Henri says, happy that the girl is commencing to speak freely.

"Please continue," Kumiko encourages. "Where is your family? Maybe we can help you find them."

"No, you can't," the girl bawls, bursting into tears with convulsions, her breath coming in large gasps as Henri takes her back into close embrace to let her weep.

"She's dead!" the girl screams.

"Your mother?"

"No, my grandmother."

"And your mother?"

"She's with father," the girl explains. "They went away when I was little. He got sick and had to go live in Yagachi Shima. Grandmother says I can't ever see them."

Henri shudders, recognizing the name of a leper colony in the north.

"Tell us your name, little one," Kumiko asks in soft voice.

"Kiyoko," she answers.

"And your family?"

"Itokazu," she answers.

"How old are you?" Kumiko asks.

"Eight," she answers.

"Now," Henri begins inquiring. "You said you know the baby Kumiko's holding. How do you know her?"

"She and her mother lived near us in Naha. Her father's a soldier and had to go away," young Kiyoko tells him.

"A Japanese soldier?"

"No. Okinawan. He hasn't been a soldier long. He used to work in Naha, but I don't know where."

The baby in Kumiko's arms is continuing to reach for Kiyoko, and the girl steps from Henri's embrace to take the baby into her arms. The baby gurgles happiness.

"What's her family's name?" Kumiko asks.

"I don't know. I just know the baby as Kanna-yoo."

"That just means darling," Kumiko says in exasperation.

"Grandmother used to babysit for her, and that's what we called her," Kiyoko explains. "I never heard her called by any other name."

Henri glances back up the road where the village elder continues to stand, glaring at them with suspicion.

"We'd better be on our way," he says to his girls.

With Kiyoko carrying Kanna-yoo with surprising ease, the little group starts down the road in the direction of the southern tip of Okinawa.

As they walk, Kiyoko seems to be mulling something in her mind and finally asks Henri, "If you're not a Buddhist priest—and being a gai-jin you can't be a priest for Mamiko, can you? What kind of priest are you?"

Henri has to laugh, knowing that in the Pedo Ko Book of Creation in the Omaru Bible, Mamiko is the goddess of the sea and created Okinawa, but he answers, "No, cheri. I'm a Christian priest. Have you heard about Jesus Christ?"

"Is it some gai-jin god?"

"You might say that," Henri explains. "He loves everyone, even you."

"I don't understand," Kiyoko says.

"You will, child, you will," Henri says, remembering that he'd always wanted to start an orphanage on Okinawa, and it seems that at last he has.

14.

Ie Shima, 1945

On the thirty-first of March, American planes come again and Yukichi spends his entire day hunkered down in a slit trench. When he emerges, he's overwhelmed by looking at a sea horizon dominated by gray silhouettes of ships in numbers he didn't think possible while the sky is filled with formations of enemy planes flying in all directions. When the wind is right, he hears faint echoes of distant explosions, and sees towering plumes of black smoke rising in the south.

Two days later he hears rumors of the American invasion at Ishikawa, and during the next week news comes of a battle on lofty Mount Yae-Take on nearby Motobu Peninsula, stark realization that the enemy is in the north. *How soon will it be before they come storming ashore on Ie Shima?* he wonders.

Events indicate it will be soon. Next day the island commander issues orders to plow up the airbase runways and then assembles the entire garrison in front of the government house in Ie. With the Japanese battle flag whipping in a spanking breeze, he steps forward and strides to a podium where he grabs a microphone and begins to address the assembly. "Soldiers of the Imperial Army and Okinawan Boetai," his voice booms over tinny speakers. "Your divine Emperor (Everyone bows in reverence before he continues) sends greetings and salutes you. Your homeland, once the ancient Kingdom of Lew Chew, has been invaded by arrogant Americans. Fear not! The valiant Thirty-second Imperial Army under the command of the honorable General Mitsuru Ushijimi stands ready to defeat them. Okinawa will be saved. This I promise. It shall require sacrifice. Death must not be a fear that deters you from crushing the enemy. Let this be our battle cry. One man for ten of the enemy or one enemy tank. I urge each of you to fight to the last flicker of your strength as you prepare to die for the Emperor."

The officer draws his sword and waves it above his head and shouts. "Banzai!"

"Banzai!" roars the assembly in answering unison. Twice more they shout the traditional cheer of the samurai, "Banzai! Banzai! Banzai!"

Yukichi turns and stares at Kozen. The officer's speech has jerked them back to a reality they'd all but forgotten. They've come to Ie Shima to die. Soon they are going to.

The Boetai are finally issued rifles and ammunition. Each guardsman receives ten bullets. There aren't enough rifles to go around, so the Japs tell the ones without rifles they must be ready to pick up one from the slain and continue the fight until they too have fallen. They issue Kozen a rifle, but not to Yukichi.

Two days later, the enemy comes ashore. As skies are turning red at sunset, Japanese regulars counter-attack, but the Boetai are held back. The moon, in its third quarter, illuminates the night and the fighting lasts until dawn. It fails, the Americans hold on to their beachhead.

Yukichi's mind is filled with a whirlwind of terrible thoughts. Nothing helps. He isn't calm, he doesn't panic, he grabs onto one thought. *I'm going to die. I'll be killed in the coming attack.* Thoughts of Kumiko and his family parents and memories of happy days of youth come flooding in. He tries to console himself with a thought of his spirit finding peace, but the strong beat of his heart, his racing pulse, and the internal heat of his face say otherwise. For two days he can't eat, but has no pangs of hunger.

Now come orders for the guardsmen to take up a position on the southern slope of Iegusugu Yama, where they wait for two days until they're told that the enemy has seized the crest of the inactive volcano. The Boetai are told to take it back!

They are herded into position, and as he looks at Kozen he watches him load his rifle. At this moment a truck drives up and parks, and all the guardsmen without rifles are told to go to the truck and pick up a weapon. Yukichi almost pukes when he learns he's supposed to a pike—a goddamned pike! The Jap bastards are sending him into battle carrying a long pole sharpened to a point at one end. *Like hell I will!* he thinks. He doesn't take anything, and returns to his previous position alongside Kozen.

While they stand there, they see a contingent of Japanese soldiers moving up to take positions in the rear. Yukichi sees Kozen's facial expression become a smirk when he locates the huge sergeant who's been abusing him.

Somebody blows a whistle and the attack begins. Soldiers carrying banners leap forward to lead the charge. Over the noise and confusion and the smell of gun smoke, guardsmen bleed and die while the wild charge up the slope continues. Yukichi sees Kozen suddenly stop, wheel, and wait until he's certain that the huge sergeant recognizes him. Kozen raises his rifle, aims and fires. A little hole appears in the sergeant's forehead and the fat bastard tumbles backwards from the killing shot.

Yukichi's sight is filled with Kozen's face, but now his eyes look directly into his own. "Sayonara, Shin'yu!" he hears Kozen yell, then sees him wheel and charge up the slope. Kozen advances but two steps before the back of his head explodes with an uplifting of black hair from the impact of a bullet.

Yukichi opens his mouth to scream, but he cannot. He hears the explosion of a mortar round and feels a terrible pressure consume his left shoulder, and everything goes black as he pitches forward and falls unconscious among the dead.

15.

In a driving rainstorm, twenty-six wounded Jap prisoners, the
only survivors from Ie Shima, lie immobile in litters stacked
like cordwood in the bed of a lurching four-by-four military
truck bound for the Prisoner Of War camp in northern Okinawa. The prisoners are drenched, feverish, and stink of mud
and blood and urine under wet woolen blankets. The truck bed
is supposed to be covered with a fitted tarpaulin, but nobody
has bothered to rig it. An armed guard assigned to oversee the
POW's avoids the monsoon downpour by going forward to
ride in the truck cab with the driver.

In a state of semiconscious state, Yukichi hasn't the
slightest idea of where he is when he comes to or even if he
has. He's not even sure he isn't dead, his soul on its way to the
Spirit World. His total awareness consists of muddled sensa-
tions dimly blurred with strange images and a feeling of wetness, faint and cold and at the same time having an inner heat
in a world of hurting, jolting motion. He's not even sure he's
awake, but the familiar sound of a whining gear train like that
he's often heard on the dredge is proof enough for his mind to
believe he's alive. There's an awareness of rain, and the weight
of his soaked blanket bears on him and hampers movement.
The discomfort of the blanket is nothing compared to the pain

consuming his left shoulder. Mustering up resolve, he tries to feel through the hurt to discover something about his injury. Gradually his mind numbs the pain, and tries to cope with a tingling feeling. *What? Something wiggling. Oh, no! Please no! Maggots.*

Panic! Dizziness! Nausea! He fights the feelings, but they come in waves across his belly. He wants to puke, but can't. His body quivers, and the nausea consumes his awareness. Almost ready to quit the fight, he's willing, even wanting, to die. He feels his eyelids flutter as blessed sleep comes.

In semi-awareness his mind accepts a dream sequence of undergoing an operation under a clear, bright light, while visions of masked faces hover over him speaking strange unrecognizable words. A sensation of his left shoulder being detached from his body while a great weight presses on him in a world without sound and strange smells of something very sweet and exceedingly clean. His mind accepts hollow reality and then returns to the security of sleep without dreams.

The return to conscious perception is a flood of bright light. Muscling his eyes shut, he keeps them that way until he's ready to trust his vision. There's something wrong with his sense of taste coming from a solid object in his mouth. He spits it out and opens his eyes and beholds a hand, a muscled pale hand intent on placing it back into his mouth. He follows the sight of the pale hand along a hairy pink arm to a face as pale as the hand. It now makes sense; the gai-jin's an American, the object is a thermometer, and this is a hospital in the camp of his enemy. Realization brings tension, even as a stab of deep pain in his left shoulder makes him go rigid and hear a buzzing sound that isn't there.

Gradually, concentration regains control of his senses, and when his head clears, he again feels stabs of hunger. He tries to ignore the thought for food, but it's no use, and hears his stomach growl. With no alternative, he becomes obsessed with what's going on with his left shoulder, so he steels himself against the pain of turning his head to examine it. What he sees is his arm and shoulder encased in gauze and tape smelling sweet enough to arouse gratitude. His mind now returns to the thought of food.

His activity prompts the American's face to come close enough to look directly into his eyes. Yukichi flashes a smile, which is not returned by the gai-jin who suddenly wraps a blood pressure cuff around his uninjured right arm, pumps it up and takes the pressure, which now causes the gai-jin to chance a hint of a smile even as he grabs Yukichi's wrist and takes his pulse. Yukichi's gaze follows the gai-jin who steps to the foot of the cot, pick up a hanging clipboard, and scribbles something before turning and walking away.

Steeling himself against the deep, deep pain in his shoulder, Yukichi looks around and tries to determine his situation. His cot is inside a large tent with canvas so new that the odor of its newness dominates the air. The floor is black earth, hard and smooth and sweating dank moisture. There's a definite impression of conscientious cleanliness invaded by mustiness. The silence of inactivity is fractured by rain falling upon the canvas and some other background noise he doesn't immediately recognize.

As he continues to look around, he's suddenly aware that there are other prisoners in the ward, lying like him on cots. All are Japanese and have bandages as white as his. Most are asleep, and those who aren't don't wave or speak as they lie motionless on their backs and stare at the canvas and listen to the rain.

Illumination is canvas-filtered daylight strengthened by a row of naked electric light bulbs hanging at even intervals from twisted green cord. He turns his attention now to faint background noise coming from outside the tent. In the near distance comes the sound of many engines. From his work on the dredger, he recalls the sound of one engine, a diesel driving an electric dynamo. The other sounds could be vehicles with laboring gear trains. Now he's aware of distant voices, strange voices shouting and yelling in words he doesn't know, but obvious the vocal tones signal frustration. There are other sounds too, sounds with which are a mystery, and these bring fear.

His investigation is cut short by the pale gai-jin's return carrying a bowl of hot broth on a tray he sets down on the medicine stand. Yukichi eyes the bowl with suspicion. His first thought is poison or maybe drugs, and he thinks that at last the murdering begins. *Why didn't they just let me die?*

As he watches, the gai-jin ladles a spoonful of broth and lifts it carefully Yukichi's lips. Even though the aroma of broth—it's obviously chicken—smells delicious, Yukichi sets his lips against the spoon entering his mouth. The gai-jin seems patient as he speaks words without meaning. "It's okay. Daijobu. Lookee here," the gai-jin says and swallows the first spoonful himself. "Daijobu—good—see."

With doubt removed, Yukichi permits the gai-jin to feed him the rest of the broth.

"More?" he hears the gai-jin ask, but he has no idea what the word means.

"Never mind," the gai-jin utters in his strange language.

"Arrigato," Yukichi says before the gai-jin departs.

The following days are spent in bed-ridden rest with occasional periods when he sits on the edge of his cot and stands for several minutes while another gai-jin replaces the cot's linen. Through it all, Yukichi has to admit that he's receiving good treatment and is eating better rations than the Japanese ever fed him. The obvious conclusion is that the Japanese stories about the savagery of the Americans isn't true. It's all so confusing.

On the morning after his counted days amount to three weeks, the gai-jin with the pale hand leads him to the front of the tent where a doctor dressed in a white smock examines his wound, removes the stitches and applies another bandage. The shoulder is still sore and seems not to have the muscular power he once had, but when he hears the doctor speak strange words, he assumes it's healing. The assumption must be correct because when the doctor finishes with him, the gai-jin doesn't return him to his cot, but leads him to another tent and leaves him in the company of other prisoners.

"Sayonara," the gai-jin says as he turns to leave.

"Sayonara," Yukichi responds and adds "Arrigato gozai masu."

"You're welcome," the departing gai-jin says with a smile, and although Yukichi doesn't know the meaning of the words, he's sure they're friendly.

In his new status as a prisoner, he's made aware that the other prisoners don't consider him their equal. It's the same old unko. The Japs are sullen and unapproachable. Part of this has to be that they've been taught that it's dishonorable to be captured. He doesn't share their belief, but he has to respect their right to believe it. While the Jap prisoners don't speak to him, he's overheard them talking among themselves about a big battle near Shuri Castle, and from this he realizes that the Americans must control the entire north of Okinawa.

Left alone, he has time to think about the future. On Ie Shima he'd prepared himself to die, but he hadn't and feels no dishonor by surviving. This war wasn't his doing, he did his duty, and that's the end of it. He's done everything asked of him, so now he has to think about what he's going to do once all this craziness ends. The obvious thing is to marry Kumiko, even if this means accepting her gai-jin religion. He'll do it. All he needs is patience. There'll be other August moons and he'll sit with his grandson, even as he sat with his grandfather. Life will go on as it always has.

Good food and moderate exercise during the following days brings a weight gain and returning strength. He has to admit he's never eaten so well. The food may be strange and oddly tasteless, but it's obviously wholesome. As to the POW camp itself, it's nothing more than a high barbed-wire fence surrounding their tent, which is isolated from the rest of the American compound.

The sights beyond the fence are astonishing. The numbers of marvelous machines with which the enemy wages war is almost unimaginable. They have trucks and vehicles of all sizes, powerful tractors, and tanks. They have enormous stockpiles of food and supplies, enough to be wickedly wasteful. What they throw away could feed a village.

As he and the Jap prisoners gain strength, they have to come to grips with another problem. One and only one prisoner is an officer. The man is silent, aloft, moody, and keeps to himself. He has a head wound, and his bandage covers his ears so he can't hear well, and he'd lost his glasses so he can't see very well either. The officer barks orders to the other prisoners just as though they were still in the Imperial Army, and he treats them all with contempt, especially this lowly Okinawan guardsman most of all.

It's wise to stay out of the officer's way, and Yukichi takes great care to do so. Things come to a head one morning when the officer shouts orders to everyone to commit hari-kari to remove the dishonor of being captured. Yukichi doesn't know what to think, and to his surprise the prisoners don't see it that way. They hold a meeting to discuss it among themselves and vote on it. What they decide infuriates the officer. Nobody considers survival a dishonor. The only reason they were captured is because they'd been wounded, and so maybe it's

Buddha's will that they live. But they inform the officer that if he wants to commit hari-kari, they'll respect his decision and even assist him if he so chooses. The officer rants and raves and curses them, but in the end he decides not to kill himself.

To Yukichi's surprise, the next day he finds himself admitted to the Jap soldier's circle of conversation. The topic concerns interrogation by the Americans, who haven't said a word about it, but according to the prisoners it's sure to come. Interrogation? This is puzzling and he says so. What could he possibly tell the enemy? After all, he knows nothing. "That will make no difference to the interrogators, Yukichi-san," one of the friendlier of the prisoners informs him. "They mean to get answers to their questions. They'll get them one way or another."

"Maybe I can make up some answers," Yukichi chances.

"You'd better be skillful if you do," advises another prisoner. "They have ways of finding out if you've lied to them."

"Yes," the first prisoner agrees. "Some of the questions they'll already have answers to. It's a kind of test, you see. It's a way of making sure you're telling them the truth, don't you see?"

"Maybe I'll just say nothing," Yukichi chances.

"In that case they'll torture you until you talk. I've heard stories about how our own interrogators do it," the second prisoner explains.

"Torture?"

"Of course, Yukichi-san," says the first prisoner. "Regardless of how well the Americans have treated us up till now, the interrogators are different. They're meaner than hell."

"But the Americans have been kind," Yukichi protests. "I've seen it."

"Who in hell shot you in the first place?"

Two days later, in the morning in a misting rain, the American interrogating teams comes for the prisoners, selecting ten at random to form five groups of two. With one American soldier leading and two others following, the group of Yukichi and the Jap officer is led single file along a path of hard packed earth that defies the rain from turning it into a quagmire. The soldiers wear rain ponchos and are armed with submachine guns. Yukichi and the Jap officer wear only cotton breeches with the letters POW stenciled on the seat in large block letters. Both prisoners feel the rain soaked breeches tug heavily at the ties and make them fear that the breeches will fall.

After several minutes the column halts before a canvas tent splotched with mildew. The lead guard halts the column, pulls back the tent's entrance flap, and motions for the prisoners to go inside. The Jap officer instantly obeys, but Yukichi holds back in fear until he feels a cold muzzle in the small of his back. He quickly follows his teamed officer into the darkness of the tent.

Tobacco smoke overpowers his sense of smell and gives him a strong urge to cough, but fear of punishment keeps him from raising his hand to his mouth. His vision adapts to the filtered daylight within the tent, and gradually interior objects come into focus, and he sees a pair of faceless silhouettes, obviously the dreaded interrogators. Their continuing silence and lack of movement unnerves him, but his urge to cough overcomes his fear. He clears his throat and coughs without raising his hand.

On a makeshift table of planks of yellow lumber supported by sawhorses, he notices several maps spread in haphazard disarray. The maps are torn, dirty, and smudged from many erasures. While working on the dredger he learned to read navigational charts, so one glance gives him recognition of the topmost map being the Motobu Peninsula. He looks quickly away, lest his interest betrays this ability to the interrogators.

Turning his attention to his interrogators, he notices that they're officers, of course, with unfamiliar insignia on their collars. One is a head taller than the other, and the taller one has a head of disheveled white hair, and it's his pipe that's the source of the offensive tobacco smoke. The smaller officer brings total surprise. He looks to be Japanese, but somehow not quite. Perhaps it's his expression, a hint of a genuine smile from a man used to smiling. And this officer begins to speak in the most beautiful and precisely correct Japanese Yukichi has ever heard.

"Gentlemen," the beautiful voice says in flawless Japanese. "I urge you to relax and stand at ease. We mean you no harm. We intend to detain you only briefly. Our main purpose is to clarify our records so that we may notify your families via the International Red Cross that you are alive and prisoners-of-war."

The beautiful voice pauses and clears its throat before continuing. "After we have verified the required information, we shall be returning you to your compound where you can once again be with your fellow prisoners. Before we go any farther, do either of you have any questions? Any complaints? Are you being treated well?"

"Nesei, neh?" Yukichi is startled to hear his fellow prisoner speak.

"Yes, I am second-generation Japanese-American," the officer with the beautiful voice acknowledges.

"Well, traitor to your race, are you enjoying your war? Your advantage is only temporary, you know," the Jap officer responds.

"I said that I am Japanese-American. I am Nisei. My parents are naturalized citizens, but American just the same," the voice defends. "I was born in the United States, so you see, I am not a traitor, as you say."

"This is more than just a war between nations," the Jap officer says. "It's a racial war: yellow against white. So you are a traitor to your race."

"We're not here to argue the point," the Nisei officer explains. "We're here to verify information in accordance with the Geneva Convention."

"Japan did not sign the stupid Geneva Convention," the Jap officer snaps.

"But the United States did," the Nisei officer counters. "The rules of the convention are binding upon the signatories—in this case, the United States."

"It's stupid," the Jap officer snarls.

Ignoring the insult, the Nisei officer continues, "Let's see: You are Lieutenant Satoru Ohno, Imperial Japanese Army, are you not? And your companion must be the Okinawan Boetai guardsman Yukichi Muragaki. Both of you were captured on Ie Shima. Are these data correct?"

"My companion, as you call him, is a mere Okinawan underling who can tell you nothing. Why do you bother?" the Jap officer says, obviously upset at hearing his name.

Steadfast in his quest for information, the Neisi continues. "We're actually more interested in what Muragaki-san can tell us than anything you know. We're after topographical information—provided, of course, he's willing to volunteer such information of his own free will."

At the word volunteer, Yukichi feels his throat tighten.

Like a bantam rooster crowing after winning a fight, the Nisei interrogator says, "You see, Satori-san, we're aware that by being captured you've already disgraced your family's name, so we know you won't talk and add to your dishonor."

Lieutenant Ohno grunts before launching into a tirade. "Filthy pig! It's you who've dishonored his family, not I. I'll wager that your father and mother and sisters are sweating in one of those notorious resettlement camps in the California dessert. Tell me it's not so, white man's lackey."

The Nisei blushes, grits his teeth, and clenches his fists as he grows silent.

Thus far, the taller interrogator has said nothing, but now he lays down his pipe, stands, and begins to speak in Japanese, "Hello, Satoru, how have you been?"

Yukichi chances a confused glance at Lieutenant Ohno and sees him smile before beginning to speak in what has to be English, "Hello, Professor Bure. I thought I recognized that smell of pipe tobacco. Long time, no see. That's what you Yanks say at times like these, isn't it?"

Yukichi sees Ohno turn to him and explain in Japanese, "Don't let this conversation confuse you, Muragaki-san. I've just discovered an old enemy."

Yukichi nods, but he's still confused.

"Enemy?" Professor Bure says, shifting the conversation back to English, which adds to Yukichi's confusion.

"Enemies!" insists Ohno. "Do you think I actually enjoyed our sick relationship? I did what I had to do to get an education. All the while, I was disgusted. I really was. You disgust me, you really do."

Whatever the words mean, Yukichi sees the taller interrogator appear to be on the verge of blushing, but it seems he's a man too sure of himself to blush. Instead he turns to the Nisei officer and includes him in the discussion, "Captain Shiguta is far too clever to fall for your lies, isn't that so, Captain?"

"Of course," Shiguta agrees, but it's plain to see he's also confused.

"There, you see," the tall interrogator states. "Captain Shiguta doesn't believe you. How did you convince yourself that I could love a mere houseboy? And a dirty yellow Jap, at that?"

"Makes you feel like a first-class American citizen, doesn't he?" Ohno asks his Nisei interrogator.

The taller American blushes and snarls, "Shut up, damn you. That's enough."

But Ohno is on a roll and continues, "Tell me, Shiguta-san, have you ever seen anybody like your round-eyed American equals? They're completely obsessed with race and sex. They're so damned afraid that somebody of a different color—yellow, black, red, or tan—is going to fuck their precious mommies. Or worse, yet, that mommy might enjoy it. Well, have you, damnit, have you?"

"Enough, I said," Bure shouts.

Frightened by the furious exchange of strange words, Yukichi moves steadily back, aware that the Japanese enlisted soldiers have told him right. The American interrogators are barbarians.

In the next instant, Ohno charges forward and begins choking the professor. Captain Shiguta runs to the tent opening and yells for the guards. The tent flap tears open and three armed soldiers rush in. If it had been only one instead of all three, they might have stopped Yukichi as he dives beneath their entangled feet, darts through the opening, and takes off running with no idea where he's heading. He hears submachine gun bursts, and sees pebbles and mud spouting ahead, behind, and beside him, but no bullets hit flesh. Up ahead he sees a steep hillside that falls away into dense vegetation and continues running until he dives headlong into it, safe from the searching bullets.

16.

Thirty-second Army Headquarters,
Shuri Castle, 1945

Takeo is drunk, stewed to the gills. He's teetering on a rain-soaked parapet while trying to piss into the wind, and not giving a damn that gusts are blowing the urine back to soil his trousers. One foot slides away, and he awkwardly recovers in the nick of time to avoid pitching forward in a neck-breaking dive into the precipitous darkness. An unsteady step backwards and he lands heavily on the packed earthen floor of the rampart.

Before him is the broad vista of territory now held by the Americans, the approaches to Shuri defenses. Poor vision conspires with the wind and the rain and the darkness to make sight hardly possible, and the fuzzy memory of throwing his glasses over the side of the parapet evokes a shout of, "Hottoke! Fuck the damned things!"

Unsteady on his feet, he slides down the wall and lands hard in a sitting position with his legs sprawled out. On his left is an empty sake bottle, one of two he's been drinking with the intention of getting drunk. It's great sake—liberated from General Cho's private stock. Near his right hand, the other bottle stands open but barely touched. He smiles and lets it become a silly giggle at the realization he's achieved the goal of coming to grips with everything that's been bothering him since he assumed his duties as aide to General Ushijimi. And it has nothing to do with the defense of Okinawa. Duty is duty, and it will be served.

Still, he's been toying with the idea of hari-kari—shooting himself and cheating the Americans out of killing him. Maybe while he's drunk he can get his pistol out and suck on the barrel until he gets the nerve to pull the trigger. Instead he looks down the barrel and asks "Anybody I know down there?" Laughing at his own little joke until tears come and he's suddenly sobbing, stopping only when he slaps himself. But a bullet is nowhere near ritual seppuku, so he holsters his pistol and swigs more sake.

"Guess what, Grandfather?" he speaks to a kindred spirit who might be with him on this rainy night, "Your little Takeo is going to get his ass shot off on this fucking island. They'll remember me as a good soldier, a hero who knows how to die for his Emperor. That's what it's all about, isn't it? That's what you taught me. I'll be united with all my fellow heroes at Yasukuni Shrine. We'll all meet there once we get killed, won't we?"

More sake, more giggles and in slurred words he says, "Maybe Hirohito himself will join us. He ought to. He's divine, you know. They say he is. Don't think so, and I know for a fact that neither does little Yoko. Remember her? Oh how I loved that girl. She's the one I should have married, but she married a banker. When we were in school she thought I was the one for her. She agreed with me even though the headmaster did his best to make us believe. Every morning we'd have to perform his little ritual. March into the courtyard and stand there while he opened a little shrine and took out a photograph of the divine one. We were expected to bow and keep quiet while he raised it over his head and expected us to adore the photo. That's when I pressed Yoko about whether she thought the Emperor is a god. But she shushed me, afraid our whispering might be found out, and both of us would get a whipping for our insolence. But I kept at it until she answered. You know, I did want to marry her and I should have, but then I went to the military academy at Zama, and she ended up marrying a damned banker."

How many times did he have to deal with this recurring memory? He doesn't know and doesn't give a damn. The memory has a way of coming back at odd times, like one of those old songs you can't get out of your mind. Come to think of it, it's reason enough for more sake. "Here's to little Yoko; Koko de sukoshi Yoshi nidesu," he slurs, taking another swig.

"Watashi ni nomanai riho? Why not drink to me?" he hears a feminine voice suddenly inquire.

He glances up and sees Cho's whore, Fumiko, standing over him. In her hand is another bottle of sake. Their eyes lock in knowing stares, and both laugh as she slides down the wall to sit close beside him.

"Ah, the sultry Fumiko," he says in gentle voice. "Kawaii desu. Koko de sukoshi Fumiko nidesu."

"Arrigato," she says and both take swigs from their bottles.

"I've had my eye on you for some time, Major," she coos.

"What about Cho-san?" he asks.

"I'm tired of having that fat old man lay on me," she says. "I want someone young and athletic—someone like you."

"Oh?"

"Yes," she says as she unbuttons his trousers and grabs his penis, which is now instantly erect.

"That feels good," he says, almost in a moan.

"Not yet," she whispers, as she opens her kimono to expose her nakedness and adds, "Mount me."

Their sex act is savage and over too soon. Takeo lays back and dozes the nap of the lion. When he awakens she is gone, and he wonders if it really happened. The disarray of his buttons and the lingering smell of their body fluids chase away any doubt. He smiles, hitches up his trousers, buttons his fly and after several deep breathes he settles into deep, peaceful sleep.

The reward of an intense headache awakens him. Groaning he slowly becomes conscious of four things. It's daylight and it's still raining and his right hand is clutching a nearly full bottle of sake and he's soaked to the skin from the rain. He vaguely remembers having sex with Fumiko and smiles at the memory as he reaches for his glasses in his tunic pocket and seems to remember throwing the damned things away during the night. He'll have to get one of the spares he keeps on hand in his quarters.

A glance at his watch brings a shout of "Oh, shit! Kusot!" Twenty minutes past eight: Colonel Harata's morning intelligence briefing is already going on! Getting to his feet takes heroic effort, but he manages to stand and now sets off to take his place. "Kusot!" he groans again, thinking how he'll waste time to stop and get the glasses. There won't be time to change uniforms; this rain soaked one will have to do.

As he takes the first unsteady step toward the parapet exit, he's startled by the sound of laughter and sees the blurred image of three soldiers who've obviously taken up their post here during the night. What they must think? A drunken officer too hung over to give a damn and too embarrassed to discipline them for disrespect is obvious. Let it go, he tells himself, so he hands the bottle to the nearest soldier and staggers through the exit and barely hears the soldier mumble arrigato.

Colonel Harata is already deep into his morning briefing, but pauses when Takeo enters the crowded briefing room. It prompts chuckles from some staff officers, but a stern glance from Ushijimi shushes them as he growls, "Glad you could join us, Major."

Takeo bows and runs to take his place behind Ushijimi's left shoulder. He hears Harata resume where he left off, and doesn't glance in Takeo's direction as he continues.

A quick study of the map's latest battle lines gives Takeo sober realization that the fighting is now beginning to assume full-scale warfare unfolding just like Ushijimi predicted. Harata's explanation of the situation is that during the time the Americans have been ashore, they've now consolidated their positions although they still haven't realized they've yet to run into the main defenses of the Thirty-second Army. Harata predicts that in another day or maybe two, they run into the positions at Kakazu Ridge, and their rapid advances will come to a halt.

Okinawa's spring weather is beginning to tell. Constant cloud cover and rains not only neutralize American air power, runoff is turning dry river beds into rushing streams with the result is that enemy troops, tanks, and armored vehicles are stuck in the mud.

As Harata explains, the entire north, including Colonel Udo's force on Ie Shima, has been lost, but this was expected. Intelligence reports that the enemy commander, General Buckner, has split his forces. The American Marines are operating solely in the north, while their Army troops are concentrated in the south. As expected, Colonel Udo's force has been annihilated; so all of northern Okinawa is lost to the Americans.

As Colonel Harata finishes his briefing, General Ushijimi reaches into his pocket and takes out a folded radio message. "Gentlemen, the IGHQ informs me that the second massed kamikaze attack will take place on April 1," he announces. "As you recall, last week's raid proved their effectiveness. They sank many enemy ships."

The reaction is nothing short of startling. Takeo hears a chorus of cheers and shouts of Banzai. The kamikazes have the American Navy reeling under their onslaught. Amid the jubilation he sees General Cho wait for a chance to put forth a daring plan.

"We should commit to an all-out attack to coincide with the kamikaze raids," General Cho proposes.

Before anyone can react, Harata shouts, "Ie! No!"

Taken aback by Harata's reaction, Ushijimi responds with, "Why not, Colonel? Wakari masen. Please explain your objection."

"Because, sir," Harata says. "It's much too early in the campaign to risk our troops in such a gamble. It's contrary to our master battle plan. Let's continue down our present road and fight a defensive fight. Besides, I don't think we'll run out of kamikaze raids, if that's the reason we're considering this one."

Ushijimi drops his gaze and mulls over the colonel's reasoning. Finally he looks up and says, "I disagree, Harata-san. I'm going to go with General Cho's proposal."

With obvious disappointment, Harata replies, "Sir, if we must, then please consider this. Let's not go all out. Let's play it safe and commit only a few shock troops. But please, sir, not what General Cho has in mind."

"No, Harata-san, my mind is made up," Ushijimi counters. "The attack will take place as General Cho proposes. We'll make it a full-scale effort."

With the noted exception of Colonel Harata, everyone is disappointed with the way things turn out. At next day's staff meeting, Ushijimi has sobering news: The IGHQ is postponing their planned kamikaze raid. Cho's big attack is called off.

17.

Shuri Castle, 1945

In the fight for Kakazu Ridge, Japanese defenders were deci-
mated by enemy air power, and nothing in Ushijimi's arsenal
could neutralize it. Their salvation comes when bad weather
grounds the enemy's planes, and it continues. Okinawa's monsoon season begins, and the first of May is a rainy day. And the
next day's the same. Pouring rain is suddenly a telling factor
in the fight for Shuri, but it doesn't seem to bother General
Buckner who orders repeated attacks even though his army
suffers heavy losses and exhausts his soldiers.

When Buckner seems convinced that Japanese defenses
are too strong to break under his relentless pressure in the rain,
he calls a halt and waits for better weather. As the American
guns grow silent, Japanese headquarters again finds reason to
celebrate. General Ushijimi is all smiles for the first time in
days, Cho is beaming, and Harata grins from ear-to-ear. "We
held them!" Cho shouts. "They threw everything they have at
us, and we held them."

"Hai! Hai!" comes an answering chorus on cue.

"Nippon is unbeatable!"

"Hai! Hai!"

"Did we kick ass?"

"Hai."

"Will we do it again?"

"Hai."

"Is this the break we've been waiting for?"

"Hai."

"Is now the time to attack in full force and chase the filthy Americans back into the ocean?"

"Hai! Hai!" the entire staff voice their approval.

Harata's smile disappears, and he grips the table so hard his knuckles turn white, as he shouts, "Iie! Never!"

Ushijimi's eyes flash surprise. Takeo continues his silence and leans forward so he won't miss a word of the gathering exchange.

"Why not?" demands Cho, hands on the hilt of his sword.

"Calm yourselves, gentlemen," cautions Ushijimi. He turns to address Harata and ask, "Yes, Harata-san, why not? Please explain. Wakari masen."

Harata pulls himself to full height and clears his throat. Aware that this will be his only shot to prevent disaster, he's fully prepared. Reason, logic, and unemotional reckoning are his weapons, and he must use them wisely.

"Our mission, indeed our entire battle plan, is to establish an invulnerable defense from which we can defeat the Americans," he says. "This is exactly what we are doing. As we know, the enemy has superior logistics; they have more men, more planes, more ships, more weapons, and more supplies and ammunition. Their resources are without end. We must also consider this: They're now entrenched in positions and the high ground we used to hold. Why will they be any less difficult to dislodge than we were? Given their strong supporting fire, the Americans will make our attack against these positions end in disaster.

"No, there should be no attack. The duty of the Thirty-second Army is to maintain the principle of a strategic holding action to the bitter end. To abandon our original battle plan now—to change our mission—would seal the fate of the Thirty-second Army. We would be crushed beneath the American heel. Also, I feel it my duty to caution you, sir, the defeat of our army means that the doors are flung open for the invasion of Nippon."

With Harata's sound argument to ponder, Ushijimi grows silent for two minutes before he turns to his chief staff officer and says, "How do you respond, General Cho?" Cho strides forward to center stage and assumes the stance of a samurai with eyes flashing fire. With great deliberation, he begins to speak. "Duty. Harata-san mentioned the word duty, did he not? Duty? I ask you, is it not our duty to die? Hai! Not a man here who doesn't know that. Put on the uniform of a warrior and you mark yourself as a man who has chosen to cross the river at the time of his lord daimyo's choosing. We wear the sword, we wield the sword, we bleed upon it, and we die young. We are men with no need of pensions, which amount to nothing but a smattering of coins for lowly civil servants. Duty means to die, means to die when and where it does the most good for the Army, for Nippon, for our Emperor, for the Nihon-jin. Let us speak no more about duty. We don't need Colonel Harata to tell us what duty means.

"What the colonel says about our strategic position is true. However, it is the reason that we must attack. Why? Because of this: What defense has ever withstood a prolonged offense by an enemy that has so many logistical advantages as the Americans? Is Shuri more impregnable than France's Maginot Line? Not at all. Not to attack means nothing more than we are besieged until we are eventually defeated. And like Harata-san says, defeat throws open the doors of invasion of Nippon. An attack, however, is a chance for victory. It's our only chance. I need not remind you that victory on Okinawa means there will be no invasion of Nippon."

Cho sits down. The room grows silent; attention now shifts to General Ushijimi, who stands with folded arms and his head lowered in deep concentration. The room is without sound except echoes of the steady beat of a single cylinder diesel dynamo and trickles of rain dripping into the cavern from interconnecting tunnels, making the air heavy and dank and smelling of mold. Finally, Ushijimi breaks his silence. "We shall attack," he announces.

Takeo's pulse quickens. Cho's samurai philosophy has prevailed. Harata shows no outward emotion, but Takeo senses the colonel's despair when he steps forward to stand before the battle map at the conference table and point his wavering finger at specific coordinates. "Our intelligence section reports that American headquarters is located here at Futema," he says. "It should be our main target. Also we have reason to believe the Americans will probably effect a relief of their front lines at 0500 hours on the fifth of May. I propose that our attack should not coincide with this time, because the enemy will be at double strength along their entire front. I also recommend that our attack force should include the Fifth Artillery Brigade to lay down an opening barrage. Other units should be the Twenty-fourth Division, the Forty-fourth Independent Mixed Brigade IMP, and the Naval Base Force."

At this moment, Takeo feels an urge to reach out and touch this man, because nobody deserves higher respect. Ushijimi and Cho must be thinking similar thoughts, because they gather around Harata and begin to plan the particulars of Cho's plan.

Using his ivory tipped cigarette holder as a map pointer, Cho starts identifying the essence of his envisioned plan. "Our attack should be a power thrust," he states. "We root our strike vector here at Shuri Castle and aim it directly at Futema, where Colonel Harata has brilliantly located Buckner's headquarters."

"I see your logic," Ushijimi says. "Cut off the head and the snake dies, all his fangs and poison useless without the brain."

"Precisely," says Cho.

"It's a sound concept," Harata agrees.

"Arrigato, Colonel," Cho says, and on this respectful note the three senior officers huddle before the map and start sorting out details.

"We need a bold opening," Harata suggests. "It should be a daring move, something to get us up and running with surprise and success."

"Agreed, Harata-san," Ushijimi states, "One good thing always leads to another. What begins well ends well."

"The question is who?" Harata asks. "What force should have the honor of launching our attack?"

"Take your pick," Cho says. "They're all fine soldiers."

"I have a unit in mind," Harata suggests. "The Second Regiment of the Forty-fourth Infantry Mixed Brigade."

"Make it so," Ushijimi orders. "General Fujioka tells me that they've already made a name for themselves. I'm impressed."

"We should talk with their commanding officer," Harata says. "He needs to know how important this first strike is and how we need complete surprise. Their objective should be to knock out American communications and upset their ability to react with our shock troops."

"Ouch!" Takeo utters, interrupting the senior officers. "General Fujioka informed me yesterday that the 44th IMB lost their regimental commander repulsing the American attack. I just now remembered, Sorry, Ushijimi-chan."

General Ushijimi winces.

"Another unit, then?" begs Harata.

"I hardly think that's necessary," Ushijimi states. "I'll tell General Fujioka to make sure the man he promotes is outstanding, and we can brief him about the mission. We can order in a replacement if Fujioka-san thinks it's necessary."

At this moment Takeo steps forward and announces, "Look no further, sirs. I'm your man. I can lead the 44th IMB into battle."

"Get serious, Major!" Cho bellows.

"No, no, let him speak," Ushijimi states. "I owe him the right to be heard."

"Arrigato, sir," Takeo says.

"Get on with it then, Major," Cho grumbles, obviously displeased, "Make your case. Let's hear it."

"Here's what I propose, sirs," Takeo explains. "I'll lead the 44th IMB's Second Regiment in an end run around the American flank and begin our attack by hitting them in the rear."

"How would you do that?" Harata asks.

"By boats, sir," Takeo answers. "The last thing the Americans expect is an amphibious landing on their flank. They're the so-called experts in amphibious warfare, but they've used them to invade and not defend against them."

"It's ingenious," Cho exclaims in surprise.

"Hah!" Ushijimi says, almost laughing. "So, the puppy wants to run with the big dogs now. That's admirable, Kuroki-san."

"You could load your troops into boats at Naha," Harata suggests, putting thoughts into words. "Proceed by night around their flank to arrive at a point behind their lines in time to launch your attack at the same time we begin our artillery barrage."

Takeo's spirit soars, and with unchecked enthusiasm exclaims, "We'll come charging ashore and start kicking ass in total surprise, sir. We'll knock out their communications and throw them in complete disarray by the time our attack begins."

"Calm yourself, Kuroki-san," counsels Ushijimi. "You still have to perform. You're signing on to great responsibility, you know? We can't support failure. If this amphibious gambit of yours is discovered, you'll not only fail, but you'll tip off our hand—meaning that the Americans will know something big is about to happen. They'll be prepared for whatever comes. That's the risk."

"That's true, sir," Takeo concurs. "But I'm up to it."

"I'm not sure I can go along with this, Takeo," Ushijimi says. "I could be out an aide, and I have no time to train a new one. There's another factor I have to consider. The troops of the 44th IMB are a cohesive unit, and they're used to their own leaders. They would resent being told to take orders from an outsider, which is what they would consider you."

"General Ushijimi is right, Kuroki-san," Cho agrees.

"We'll discuss this later," Ushijimi says. "Just now, we have many details to decide before we have to consider your request, noble as your intentions are."

Takeo's spirit sank as he starts having doubts about taking part in the attack. For the remainder of the planning session, he stands in complete silence, a perfect observer. As details unfold, he begins to understand what Ushijimi means. The stakes are enormous. Ushijimi intends to make this gambit all-or-nothing. Either we will defeat the Americans or suffer our own defeat. The objective is simple—total destruction of Buckner's Tenth Army.

At one point in the planning, Ushijimi hands Takeo a radio dispatch to take to the staff communications officer for encoding and transmitting to the IGHQ in Tokyo. The message requests a massed kamikaze attack of as many planes as they can put in the air. Request? Hell, he has to have them. It also specifies that the Thirty-second Army's attack will begin on the night of May 3.

Thirty minutes later they have their answer. The IGHQ agrees to mount a two-day maximum kamikaze effort to support the attack. The plan is now etched on steel. As they're wrapping up details, Ushijimi breaks away from the group and makes eye contact with his aide. "Fifteen minutes—in my quarters, Kuroki-san."

"Hai, domo," Takeo responds.

Quarter of an hour later, Ushijimi sits at his desk and says, "Have a seat, Takeo." Takeo obeys and leans forward to await the verdict.

"I'm not at all happy about this matter," Ushijimi says. "If I let you go, I risk losing you. And if I don't, there's risk that the new regimental commander of the 44th IMB might not be up to the task, which means that our attack could get off to a bad start. I need assurance that this man is fully aware of what's expected and knows how important this mission is. Do you understand what I'm saying, Takeo?"

Takeo nods.

"Here's what I've decided to do," Ushijimi states. "I'm not going to turn the regiment over to you, but I am going to send you to judge whether this officer, whoever he is, has the courage, dedication, and presence of mind to carry it off. You're to go to Naha and see for yourself that what needs to get done will be done. You're to be my eyes and ears on this, and I'm giving you full authority to take command if in your judgment it needs to be done. If you think the new commander is capable and has been properly briefed, then let him go without any interference from you or anyone else. Is this clear? Do you understand what's expected of you?"

"Hai, domo," Takeo says and stands and bows.

"One last thing," Ushijimi states, handing him a written note giving him authority to relieve the new commander—if need be.

Takeo pauses at the door. "Be careful, son," he hears Ush-ijimi say.

The second wave of kamikazes shows up during the morning before the attack. They're equally effective as the previous day, sinking several warships and putting an aircraft carrier out of action. When darkness falls, the kamikazes are used up.

During the afternoon Kuroki makes arrangements to rendezvous and when daylight is gone, he's approaching the 44th IMB at the waterfront in Naha. Troops are already loaded into barrages. A smallish spit of an officer stands waiting on the pier and glances at his watch as though Takeo is tardy even though it's not yet time to shove off. there's still fifteen minutes before shove off. "Major Kuroki-san, I'm Major Matsuki," the officer says, bowing.

"Let's dispense with formalities," Takeo commands.

"Arrigato," Matsuki-san agrees.

"Have you been briefed?"

"Hai, by General Fujioka himself."

"Tell me, Matsuki-san, what's expected of you?"

"To circle the American flank, land behind their lines at Kuwan and attack precisely at fifteen minutes after midnight," Major Matsuki recites. "If we're early, then our cue will be the start of our artillery barrage, which I can hear. Once we're ashore, we're to attack their communications facilities and their headquarters. To engage enemy troops is not our primary objective. Is this your understanding of my mission, sir?"

"It is," Takeo concurs.

"Anything else, Major?" Matsuki asks.

"Just one thing, Major," Takeo inquires. "What do you plan to do after the war?"

"Fuzaken na?" Matsuki-san says with a laugh. "Are you fucking kidding me? I'm going to meet you and everybody else on this island at Yasukuni Shrine. Whether tonight or to-morrow or next week, I'm not going to survive this war. Just like you, Major, I'm going to die for Nippon, and like you, I'll have no regrets."

"Sayonara, Matsuki-san," Takeo says. "Until Yasukuni."

When Takeo gets back to Shuri, he hears Ushijimi say, "I'm happy to see you're back, Kuroki-san. I presume that you found the new commander acceptable."

"Tak-san," Takeo smiles.

"Disappointed?" ventures Ushijimi.

"Skoshi," Takeo admits. "But the man is worthy. He won't disappoint us."

As Takeo reads the battle reports as they filter into Thir-ty-second Army Headquarters, the attack begins with disap-pointment. The amphibious end run runs into rotten luck. American Marines are waiting and take them under fire while the barges are still heading for the beach. Every man of the 44th IMB force is killed.

Precisely fifteen minutes after midnight, Japanese artillery commences a thunderous barrage. But the enemy is up to the challenge, and the exchange of big guns lights up the darkness. All through the night and well into the morning hours, artil-lery on both sides exchange fire. When noon comes, Japanese artillery have suffered terrible losses and grows silent. Despite expending thousands of rounds, they haven't dislodged the Americans from a single position.

In the furious night, Cho's main force attacks. The battle loses structure and becomes a massive armed brawl, each man for himself. Opposing soldiers shoot at shapes, shadows, any-thing making motion. The fighting ebbs and flows, impossible to tell which side is winning or if either side is winning.

What little armor Ushijimi has left, he commits to the attack. There are early claims of success, but these prove false and so the tanks suffer the same fate as the artillery. Every tank is destroyed.

At dawn the weather clears, and enemy planes take to the sky and strike with rockets and napalm. Cho's attack jars to a halt, wavers, and retreats. Failure! Defeat! As dusk envelopes the battlefield, seven thousand Imperial soldiers lay dead upon the killing fields. The enemy controls the battlefield.

Ushijimi turns to Colonel Harata and sobs, "You were right, Hiromichi-san. I should have followed your advice and not consented to this attack. Why didn't I see it? Why? Why? From now on, I shall follow your recommendations like a schoolboy." Colonel Harata does not reply—what can he say? Like everyone else, he knows all they can do now is crawl back into the Shuri defenses and await the inevitable.

It's General Cho who puts the cap on the event. "We must abandon all hope for victory on Okinawa. Only time stands between us and annihilation."

Takeo weeps. Samurai though he is, he weeps.

18.

Southern Okinawa, 1945

The rainy season turns the south green, and into this lush farm-land come four exhausted refugees—Henri, Kumiko, and little Kiyoko carrying Kanna-yoo. In total exhaustion, they plod along the road leading to the edge of the high plateau over-looking the sea, realizing that here they'll have to pause and follow the shoreline either east or west. But before they reach the coast, they have to make a decision. Rather than making one, Henri kneels and prays for guidance.

Kumiko's patience is at its end. Although she loves her Pere-san sans aucun doute, in this situation she can no longer suffer his piddling ways. Enough is enough, and this is enough. Here, in the middle of this unfamiliar road with the sun about to set and the smell of rain heavy in the air, Pere-san is praying. Praying! "Pere-san!" she screams. "You have to find us a place to spend the night."

Henri crosses himself and looks sharply up from his kneeling position. He's getting more than a little sick and tired of her nasty voice, and he's ready to do something about it here and now. "Young lady—" he begins as he's rising to his feet.

"Don't young lady me!" she interrupts. "You know what we need. You're not only a shisai, you're also a man. Act like it! Find us a place to stay—"

"But…"

"…before it rains," she concludes while turning and walking away, leaving him to purse his lips and look around.

The shelter he finds is a gan beside the road. At first Kumiko isn't pleased by imposing upon the dead, but she stops grumbling when she compares it to camping again in the open, especially now that light rain is falling.

She turns her attention to food, especially for the children. Foraging and gleaning are arts yet unfamiliar, but Kumiko realizes it's something they'll have to learn. But this night they bed down in the gan with pangs of hunger.

During the night the rain stops, and dawn sees them rise and quickly abandon the tomb. After cleansing themselves, they're on the road again heading south. The coast has to be near; they can smell the sea.

When they reach the coast, they come to a fork in the road. Each branch follows the coastline. Signposts point to the left for the towns of Guchichan and Minatoga, and to the right is the village Hanagusuku.

"Which way?" Henri asks Kumiko.

"Beyond Minitoga is the Chinen Peninsula on the Pacific Ocean," she says. "I think we should go that way."

"But the sea cliffs on the coast look so high," Henri says. "Wouldn't that make finding refuge difficult?"

"I don't think it makes any difference," she reasons. "There are cliffs in both directions. I think it makes more sense to go toward Chinen."

"But first there's Minatoga. Perhaps they'll let us stay there."

"After what happened at Iwa, we shouldn't count on it," she states. "These people are going to be suspicious of you."

"I should let you go on alone with Kiyoko and—" he starts to say.

"Don't be ridiculous, Pere-san!"

"But—"

"No buts," she says, cutting him off. "We stay together!"

"If you say so," he concedes. "Merci, ma cheri."

"There's a chance you could be right," she says. "Why don't you stay here and take care of Kanna-yoo while Kiyoko and I go to Minatoga and see if they're more hospitable than the farmers at Iwa?"

"I could use the rest," he says.

"That too," she says.

"God be with you," he says, but the two girls are already on their way, Kumiko leading with Kiyoko running to keep up.

In a mood to see the sea, Kumiko abandons the road and decides to walk along the grassy edge of the high cliffs where there's a stiff breeze blowing over a sweeping panorama of the southern coast. In several minutes they're out of sight of her guardian and making slow but deliberate progress. Up ahead they see a lone soldier, a sentry standing at his post. No other soldiers are in sight.

"Come," she says. "We'll go back to the main road."

"Halt!" the sentry calls and levels his rifle at them.

They freeze.

"State your business," the sentry orders.

"We have no business," Kumiko tries to explain.

"Then what are you doing here?"

"We're fleeing Naha. It's being destroyed," Kumiko says and starts to walk away.

"Come here!" the sentry growls.

"No!" Kumiko objects.

"I said come here, and I won't repeat myself," he says, aiming his rifle.

Kumiko hesitates, but then starts to obey, even as she's whispering to Kiyoko, "Run back to Pere-san."

"No!" Kiyoko says and falls into step beside Kumiko. They soon reach the edge of the sea cliff where the soldier stands waiting.

"What do you want?" Kumiko asks. "We've done nothing."

"What do I want?" the sentry says. "You're a beautiful girl—even for an Okinawan. What does any lonely soldier want from a beautiful young girl?"

"I'm not that kind of girl, a yariman," Kumiko declares.

"All Okinawan girls are that kind," the sentry says as he sets his rifle down and reaches for Kumiko. She turns to escape, but he grabs her wrist and pulls her to him.

"Leave her alone!" Kiyoko screams.

"Shut up, little girl," the sentry says. "You could be next."

Kumiko starts to struggle, but the sentry's grip is too tight to break away. He grabs her around the waist and throws her down upon the grass. Then he starts unhitching his trousers, readying himself to take his pleasure.

Kiyoko grabs a handful of pebbles and throws them at him. One pebble strikes him in the eye.

Enraged, the sentry yells "I'll get you, you meinu nidesu!"

By now Kiyoko has located a larger stone and hurls it at the sentry. It hits him in the forehead, forcing him to back away, lose his footing, and tumble over the edge of the cliff. He screams in terror as he plummets to his death.

Kumiko gets to her feet, grabs the sentry's rifle and tosses it over the cliff. She grabs Kiyoko by the hand and starts leading her away, back toward the main road.

"Monshi wakenai!" Kiyoko blubbers. "I didn't mean to kill him. I've never killed anybody. I just wanted to make him stop hurting you."

"Never mind. Kinishinade!" Kumiko says.

Kiyoko breaks into tears, but Kumiko tells her, "You did what you had to do. Forget it. You're a brave little girl."

Returning to the main road, they start back to where Henri sits resting.

"You're back already?" he asks as they approach.

"Yes," Kumiko replies. "We must go the other way. It's not safe this way."

"What happened?" Henri demands.

"Nothing," Kumiko says. "We could see that it's not safe. We need to go in the other direction."

"Toward Hanagusaku, you mean?" he asks, getting to his feet and handing Kanna-yoo to Kiyoko.

"Yes," Kumiko replies. "To the west."

A hard trek brings them to Hanagusuku where they find Japanese soldiers forcing the townsfolk to evacuate before their homes are set on fire. Continuing on, they finally come to the next village, Nakaza. It's a scene similar to Hanagusuku, with more soldiers preparing to burn the town. As they approach town center, the sergeant in charge beckons for Henri to come here. "You're a gai-jin holy man, are you not?" the sergeant demands.

"I'm Christian—a Roman Catholic priest, a shisai."

"Where are you going?"

"We don't know," Henri says. "My ward and I are fleeing from Naha."

"You have children," the sergeant observes.

"Orphans," Henri replies.

"Orphans? You want orphans?" the sergeant inquires.

"We don't need more orphans, if that's what—," Kumiko starts to break in.

"Quiet, woman! You will take some orphans," the sergeant barks. "In that house over there are several children. You go and tell the soldier you're there to take custody."

"We'd be happy to take them, only we have no way to transport them or feed and care for them," Henri objects, speaking for Kumiko.

"I will provide a handcart and two bags of gohan," the sergeant proclaims.

"Utensils and pots?" Kumiko asks in the humblest of voices.

"Scavenge what you can, but take the children and leave. And don't go to Itoman! Go southwest. We're fortifying the hills to the north," the sergeant says, before shouting to one of his soldiers to fetch the handcart and provisions.

"But the southwest is the sea," Kumiko objects.

"There are caves along the shore where you will be safe," the sergeant explains.

"Hai, domo," Henri replies and bows to the sergeant, who's now walking away.

A soldier soon returns with the promised handcart and bags of rice. Henri and Kumiko set off for the designated house, leaving Kiyoko to watch their new possessions while tending to Kanna-yoo. In the house they find a soldier happy to be relieved of his babysitting duties. Before leaving, he points to a komado on which there's a pot of warm fish stew and rice.

The waifs are four, all girls. The youngest is an infant, no more than a day old when she was abandoned by her mother, and that's all any of the other children can tell them. There's one infant about a year old, and the other two girls are both pre-teens capable of helping Kumiko care for the infants, now three in number.

Henri scarfs down several mouthfuls of stew before setting off to relieve Kiyoko at the handcart. Kiyoko is excited to learn there's fish stew waiting and sets off with the baby to get nourishment. In no time, it seems, she and Kumiko return with the other girls, each carrying an infant.

"The soldier came back," Kumiko says. "He said we have to leave the house immediately because his orders are to put a torch to it. He did let us take the food. Before we left he extinguished one of the torches and gave it to me."

"Don't we still have lucifers?" Henri asks, recalling that Kumiko used one to make a fire last evening.

"I did, but they got wet," Kumiko says. "To be on the safe side, I brought a flint, steel, and tender box. We can make fire."

Quick not to overstay their welcome, they set off and follow the road until it ends on the other side of town. It brings them to another decision. Disregarding what the sergeant told them, they decide to head south. Making good time, now that they have a handcart, they soon come to a farming hamlet called Mabuni. All houses were deserted, and there's no sign of life, meaning that the farmers must have taken their animals and poultry with them. Although there are no soldiers, Kumiko gets an eerie feeling they're being watched.

After Mabuni, they find themselves pushing their handcart around the base of a high hill until just before sunset they come to a precipice, a high cliff overlooking the sea. Their problem is how to get down to the shore; the descent is perilous. In the struggle, they almost lose the handcart with its precious load before they stand at last at the edge of the sea.

Exhausted yes, but they have the comfort of knowing they'll be able to eat, and so they build a fire and camp under a starry sky. While Henri says his vespers, Kumiko has to give in to sleep, leaving the awed girls pretending to be brave enough to handle a situation demanding courage, and now bone-aching weariness lets them sleep.

They awaken to tragedy. The infant is dead. They weep, but do not wail. As the sun comes up, Kumiko assembles the children and shushes them while Henri opens his missal to the prayer of death. "Saints of God," Henri prays in Latin. "Come to her aid! Come to meet her, Angels of the Lord. Into your hands, O Lord, we humbly entrust our sister. In this life you embraced her with your tender love; deliver her now from every evil and bid her rest. The old order has passed away; welcome her to paradise, where there will be no sorrow, no weeping or pain, but fullness of peace and joy with your Son and the Holy Spirit forever and ever. O God, by whose mercy the departed find rest, send your holy Angel to watch over this grave. Through Christ our Lord. Amen."

To the girls Henri's Latin sounds like gibberish, but they remain respectfully silent as Kumiko scoops out a shallow grave and buries the baby beside the sea, and nobody knows her name. They mark the grave with a stone—all they can find. They get back to the task of surviving.

This section of the coastline has natural caves, and Kumiko faces the fact that cave living is being forced upon them. She sits down and ponders her alternatives. The one thing she knows is that the decision will be hers and hers alone; Pere-san will have no say in this. Luck is with her. Pere-san is busying learning the girls' names.

The first thing she wants—demands—is that the cave entrance and floor must be higher than the highest high tide—in other words, a dry cave. Remembering something Yukichi told her about the sea he'd learned while working on the dredger, she realizes she has to look at watermarks left on the rocks to get what she wants. The next thing has to be ventilation, not only for breathing but also for building a fire within the cave. A fire means smoke, and this brings her to the need for a natural chimney. And it would be nice to have a hidden entrance, but this is probably asking too much.

With these matters in mind, she sets off exploring to see what the shoreline has to offer. Luck or Providence—whichever—is with her. Within the first hour she stumbles upon the ideal cave, and she knows in an instant it's meant to be hers; the cave entrance is hidden so well, she's the first person to discover its existence. Saying a prayer of thanksgiving, she crosses herself and goes running to tell Pere-san where they're going to live while waiting for the war to end.

19.

Shuri Castle, 1945

"I've never been in such wind!" Colonel Harata shouts to Takeo in the midst of a furious night storm, and even with his hands cupped he's unable to make himself understood. Cracking thunder from successive bolts of lightning drowns out all attempts of conversation in the parapet overlooking the battleground. Rumbles of the ongoing American artillery barrage are no match for the thunder and sweeping rain.

All Takeo can do is shake his head. Not only is he unable to hear, he can't see either. Smeared by spray from the rain, his useless glasses are now inside his tunic pocket. He's relieved when Harata-san shakes his head and starts for the tunnel entrance.

Out of the weather, the operations officer begins, "This weather is our best ally, Kuroki-san, but it's not enough."

Takeo wipes his glasses, puts them on, and reacts to colonel Harata's puzzling remark. "But isn't it what we wanted?"

"Yes, of course," Harata continues. "The weather suits our purpose—but not enough to make up for the way the battle is going."

"I was under the impression that fighting while concentrated inside our defenses was our plan."

"You just said the word," Harata states.

"What word, Harata-san? Wakari masen—I don't understand, sir."

"Concentrated," Harata says.

"Concentrated?"

"We're too concentrated," Harata explains. "As our troops give way, we've doubled back on ourselves until we've become too concentrated. The Americans have freedom to wheel, maneuver and react, and we don't. The result is that everywhere they hit us, they hurt us."

Takeo nods understanding and follows with, "What's the solution?"

"That's why we're here."

"Wakari masen."

"I'm recommending we pull out to the south to gain mobility. If we don't, we're going to collapse."

"Have you discussed this with Generals Ushijimi and Cho?"

"I have," Harata answers.

"And...?"

"We've decided to abandon Shuri and withdraw."

Shocked, Takeo grits his teeth and says nothing.

"Ushijimi-chan wanted me to inform you first hand," Harata explains. "He doesn't want you to be surprised when he informs the staff at tonight's conference.".

"Arrigato, Harata-san."

"I can tell from your expression that you think the staff officers aren't going to like this decision," Harata says. "Especially the corps commanders—and General Fujioka in particular. His 62nd Division has suffered most of all."

"What about the wounded?" Takeo says. "We have hundreds in the hospital. They won't be able to travel. They'll die."

"They'll die anyway, Takeo-san," the colonel argues. "We all will. It's only a question of when and where. When we came to Okinawa we all knew we'd be giving our lives for the Emperor and Nippon. As General Cho has said many times, a soldier can't ask for more. For once, I have to agree."

At the staff meeting, Takeo sees Harata's prediction is correct. The room is silent except for the background noise from the storm raging outside and occasional fall of a pebble caused by earth vibrations from relentless American artillery. After Ushijimi's surprise announcement, Colonel Harata takes over the meeting, wasting no time in explaining the current tactical crisis and what they're going to do about it. He ends his remarks by stating there will be no questions and no discussion.

During the briefing Takeo stands silently behind his general, and is startled when he's suddenly aware of the putrid smell of his daimyo's obvious hyperventilation. He exchanges a concerned glance with the general, who flashes a grin of embarrassment before looking away. Nevertheless Takeo feels a stab of fear about the possibility of heart attack, and he breathes a sigh of relief when Ushijimi straightens his posture.

When Harata finishes, Cho takes the floor and begins explaining how they plan to accomplish what has to be done. "Our withdrawal has to be made in absolute secrecy, " he says. "If the goddamned Americans get any inkling of what we're up to, they'll jump on us like fleas on a dog. All preparation—packing, stowing, transpiration, document destruction, troop assembly—every last thing about this operation has to be done with the utmost secrecy, silence, and security. Logistic support will begin immediately and be completed as soon as possible. For obvious reasons we haven't set a time yet for the first truck convoy to get underway. However, we're looking at a time window starting in about twenty-four hours. The weather will play a role in choosing the time, of course, and it looks safe to expect the storm to continue."

Officers whispering in the background causes Cho to yell, "Silence! Pay attention. Now, it's obvious that we're going south to take up prepared positions in the Yuza Dake hills on the Kiyamu Peninsula. It's good terrain, and we'll make the Americans bleed as they try to dig us out. We've established reserve ammunition dumps throughout Yuza Dake, so supplies and ammunition will be no problem."

Cho pauses to let his words sink in, and this time he doesn't say anything about the whispering. "So much for our end game," he continues. "Now for our board strategy: It's bold, and it involves our rear guard, who will be our knight that can move and wheel and slash and kill as they fight a delaying action. Their assignment is to hold the Americans at bay without tipping our hand. Fortunately, we have the best in General Fujioka's 62nd Division. We realize that they have already sustained many casualties and are now a shadow of what they were in their prime, but their spirit is strong as ever and will hold off the Americans until May 29. Then they will abandon Shuri and fall back to the Kokuba River, where they will regroup and continue fighting their delaying action until June 2. On that date they will turn and dash south to rejoin us. Since there are no questions, General Ushijimi will have the last word. General..."

Takeo watches Ushijimi advance two small steps to center stage, and tries to understand how the general must feel. He hopes the strain of accepting the need to retreat has eased, but nevertheless he knows that Ushijimi must address his loyal staff officers. As he listens to Ushijimi begin to speak, he knows the general's on the verge of tears. No wonder; it's probably the last time he'll look at the assembly of his loyal staff officers. "I am ordering the withdrawal to begin tomorrow afternoon before dark," Ushijimi says. "There will probably be continued rain and storms to cover our movements. As General Cho has explained, the exact hour will be announced later. I am fully aware of the sacrifices and contributions each of you has performed. You have been magnificent. I thank you. I'm sure the Emperor thanks you. You are dismissed."

Takeo can't believe what he's just heard. *This was the whole of the speech? Those were all the words? Where was the inspiration? Where was the spirit?* Takeo can hardly control his emotions, and he sets his jaw to keep from blurting out how he feels, but, oh, how he hurts for General Ushijimi.

Takeo notices Ushijimi nod and mumble something he can't quite understand.

"Sir...?"

Ushijimi glares, clearly annoyed. "What I said, Major Kuroki, was for you to accompany me to my quarters. I have some dispatches I want you to help me prepare."

"Hai domo," Takeo answers. "I'm sorry, sir, I didn't hear."

"It's not your fault, Takeo," Ushijimi says, before beginning to shuffle towards the exit. "I'm not myself today. Come, we need to talk. I have some things to settle."

"Of course, sir," Takeo answers, falling in behind his commander.

"Come walk beside me, Takeo," Ushijimi says, speaking in halted phrases. "We'll walk together like we did in Tokyo. Do you remember that morning, son? We were going to catch the plane and you were telling me about your grandfather's sword. Then we flew over Fuji-san. It looked so beautiful in the bright sunlight. We flew into a cloud and it disappeared. I remember like it was yesterday."

"Hai, domo," Takeo replies. "It was a happy time."

In the privacy of his quarters, Ushijimi sits down heavily and begins to stare as though he was musing days of long ago glories. Then he sighs and begins thinking out loud, "I do believe, Takeo-san, that my commanders don't want to face this thing, even though we've known it was coming. Knew it had to come, as surely as the sun sets and darkness takes over the night. Know what I mean?"

"I think I do, sir."

"Yes, of course you do," Ushijimi rambles. "Your grandfather taught you well. From what you've told me, I believe he was cheated. It was probably why he hated Emperor Meiji. As samurai we live our lives thinking that we'll never have to face the lengthening shadows. We think we'll lose our sight of the sun at high noon when a cloud blocks out the light, and the next time we see the light we'll be at Yasukuni. Now that cloud is approaching. I'm not afraid, but I admit to being nervous."

"We all are, sir."

"I have an assignment for you, Kuroki-san," the general says. "I'm certain that you'll perform it with the same excellence you usually do."

"Arrigato, sir. You make it easy to serve you."

"Do I now?" Ushijimi says, flashing a smile before reverting to seriousness.

"Yes, sir. Always."

Ushijimi continues, "On the extreme southern coast near the village of Mabuni is a crag overlooking the sea. It's a forbidding place, a rugged hill. Some months ago, General Cho had his engineers fashion an underground complex, which will soon become our new command post—my final command post. Your task is to transfer the nucleus of my headquarters staff and our communications center to this new site. Any questions?"

"None, sir. It will be ready when you want it."

"I'll give you my timetable," Ushijimi explains. "Our garrison is going to commence the move tomorrow afternoon before dark on May 23rd. All units except General Fujioka's rear guard should complete re-deployment five days later on the 28th. I plan to shift my command to Mabuni just as soon as you complete your assignment. I should like this to be no later than the 25th. This is your schedule."

"I will make it so, sir."

"Good," Ushijimi says. "You can go now, but as you leave would you please inform Generals Cho and Fujioka, who are waiting outside, to come in."

"Hai, domo."

"I have bad news for them," Ushijimi explains. "Fujio-ka-san expressed some concern about transportation for the wounded, and I have to tell him that except for the slightly wounded, they can't go. Those who've given the most cannot go. There is no time, no facilities, no transportation."

"Wakari mas, I understand."

"It's good that you do, Major. It's going to be asked of you, too."

"I'll be ready, sir."

"I believe you will, Takeo," Ushijimi says. "Our grandfathers raised us well."

Takeo takes leave and after informing Generals Cho and Fujioka that Ushijimi is waiting to receive them, he turns and is surprised by a medical orderly who's obviously been waiting some minutes to see him.

"Major Kuroki-san?" the orderly says.

"Hai."

"Sir, we have a wounded man in the hospital requesting an audience with you. Can you come, sir? He's unable."

"Who?" Takeo asks in total surprise.

"Corporal Koya, sir. The man said his name is Koya. He's in the 62nd Regiment."

"Koya-san? I don't recall knowing any Koya-san."

"He told me he didn't think you would, sir, but it seems that it has something to do with a bottle of sake," the orderly explains. "That's all he said."

"Sake? Wakari masen," Takeo says, recalling his drunken awakening in the parapet. "Oh, now I remember. Corporal Koya must have been one of—"

"Pardon, sir, but there's not much time. Koya-san is severely wounded, and I'm needed back at the hospital. If you would be so kind…"

"Of course," Takeo agrees and follows the lead of the orderly.

The trip is a short walk through the underground passages to a large cavern serving as the hospital for the 62nd's wounded soldiers. As they near the stench becomes stronger and stronger until he's ready to gag. "How do you stand the smell?" Takeo asks.

"I don't know, sir. I guess you get used to it."

"Is there something I can take?"

"Sorry, sir. And even if there were, I don't think we'd have it."

Takeo steels himself to the odor, and just when he thinks he can handle it, they arrive at the entrance of the hospital cavern, where the odor hits his nose like a hammer, forcing him to bend over and grunt in order not to puke.

"Are you all right, sir?" he hears the orderly ask, and then he hears another voice beckon "Orderly!"

Takeo straightens and sees a frantic medical officer who has the look of a man trying to deal with an emergency of some sort.

"Come quickly! I need you," the officer insists, then waves and is gone.

"Sorry, sir. that was my superior. Orders, sir. I must obey. I have to go."

"Don't leave me," Takeo pleads. "Tell me where this Koya-san is."

"Over in that area," the orderly shouts just before he disappears from view.

Takeo shrugs his shoulders and begins an aimless search.

He finds the sights as bad as the smell. Admitting he hasn't thought about it, but the wounds inflicted by American weapons are worse than anything he'd ever known in China. The wounds of this battle shock his senses and tear his previous imagination to bits. The pain of these soldiers must go all the way to their brain's reptilian core.

Accepting the task at hand, Takeo begins searching in a logical sequence of going up and down the rows of litters laid out so as to separate the living from the dead. His search seems fruitless; there doesn't seem to be a Corporal Koya among the living, and if the soldier is dead, it won't matter. As much as he hates it, he's ready to give up. He has Ushijimi's task at hand, and time is precious.

"Major Kuroki, sir," Takeo hears a labored whisper say, and he wheels and starts him to try and locate the summons.

"Over here, sir," he hears the whisper again, coming from an area of darkness.

Kuroki walks in the direction the whisper came from, and suddenly he locates it in a dark recess. "Koya-san?" Takeo asks a prone figure sheathed in a mass of filthy bandages covering his face, arms, hands, and upper torso. Koya-san is a pair of eyes gazing up at him from behind a bandage mask; he has the stench of dried, oozing puss on stiffened gauze. Takeo tries to flash a smile—and perhaps he does. He can't be sure.

The whisper speaks again. "Domo arrigato," it says. "It's good of you to come."

"Kombam wa, Koya-san," Takeo greets. "Do I know you?"

"I don't think so, sir. But you showed us some kindness once. And everyone knows of Major Kuroki, aide to General Ushijimi."

"Kindness? You mean the sake—in the parapet in the morning in the rain. I was not at my best, I'm sure you noticed."

Koya tries to laugh, but the pain is too much.

"It was magnificent sake, sir. None of us had ever tasted such fine wine. At first we started to swig it, but it was so delicious that we saved it and shared with our comrades. We heated it just as they do in the best geisha houses and sipped it."

"If I may ask, what is your full name, Koya-san?" Takeo asks.

"Taro, sir. Taro Koya," he answers. "I come from the village of Nagai near Kamakura. You've heard of the great Daibutsu Buddha?"

"I know Kamakura well, Taro-san," Takeo replies. "And Nagai too. It's on Segami Wan with a beautiful view of Fuji-san. We have a military airfield there."

"Hai, that's it."

"You had two friends with you in the parapet, I believe. Do you know how they're getting along?"

"Dead, sir. Both died honorably in the service of the Emperor. They were good soldiers, sir. Always we kept trying, never thinking about giving up no matter how hard the going got. We continued to believe that we would crush the Americans. We dug our caves thinking they might be our graves. Nakamura—you might remember him as being the tallest—was the first to be killed. We were defending Dakeshi when his position took a direct hit from an artillery shell. Suddenly there was just no more of him."

"And the other man?" Takeo prompts.

"He was the laughing one. He was Hidari-san. He died very nobly. He really did. You would have been proud of him, sir."

"I'm sure I would."

"We were being attacked by tanks, sir," Koya continues. "About twenty of them. Our officers called for artillery, but it was too little and they couldn't find the range. The tanks had to be stopped, sir. We had nothing but satchel charges, explosives that had to be delivered by hand. Hidari and I were a team. We had one satchel between us. We made a coordinated attack. Hidari darted in front of the tank, diverting fire from their machine gun. In the confusion of Hidari's attack, the enemy didn't notice my approach. I placed the satchel charge and rolled away to take cover in a small hole. Then Hidari went down—hit I'm sure. The tank rolled on, crushing him. His belly burst like a pimple. Then the charge exploded, destroying the tank. Goddamn them, sir. I killed them. I killed them all. I'm glad I killed them—for what they did to Hidari-san."

Koya is suddenly in convulsions. The puss and the blood start to flow from his filthy dressings. He doesn't notice and goes on with his story.

"I was scared to death, sir," he continues. "All I could think of was to run. I stood and started running. I don't know where. I was so afraid. All I remember is that I just made it back to our bunker, and suddenly there was another tank like a big steel monster in front of me. It slowly swung its ugly turret until all I could see was the burning black hole of its napalm nozzle. It's inhuman, sir. I couldn't take it. I broke and ran. I ran! I was a coward. I tried to fight well, sir, I honestly did. But to face that fire, that horrible fire…"

While Koya sobs, Takeo pulls himself erect and goes in search of a medical officer. "Doctor," he orders, when he finds one. "I want morphine—a lethal shot."

A weary pair of puzzled eyes returns his stare.

"There is a soldier over there," Takeo explains. "I know him. He's a hero. He is suffering too much. He's going to die anyhow, but I want to spare him further agony."

"Major, I would like to oblige," the doctor says. "I really would. But there is no morphine. There's nothing. We have nothing."

"Anything," Takeo pleads.

"Only this," the doctor answers, handing him a bloody scalpel.

"Shouldn't we clean it?" Takeo asks.

"Major, does it really matter?" the doctor says and walks away, leaving Takeo to stare after him.

Takeo glances at the bloody scalpel for only an instant, then strides back to where the wounded hero lies. He kneels down beside Koya-san, takes a breath and looks into the eyes behind the gauze mask. He sees them stare first at the scalpel blade and then dart back to match Takeo's gaze. Taro blinks twice and nods agreement.

"It won't hurt. I know the seppuku stroke. You won't feel a thing."

"Do it, sir. I can't stand the pain. Please do it! Do it now."

Takeo grits his teeth, sets his mouth, places the blade at the precise angle and the precise point below the rib cage to thrust into the heart without impediment. Looking into Taro's eyes he thrusts the blade home. Taro makes no cry, he matches Takeo's gaze until the light goes out of his eyes. Takeo stands and salutes, then turns and with tears blurring his vision, hurriedly strides from this chamber of death.

20.

Preparations for moving Ushijimi's headquarters turn out not to be the difficult task Takeo envisioned. It's quite simple really. There's surprisingly little to move. Most of what occupies current headquarters turns out to be non-essential military bric-a-brac, which he merely discards. The communications people have their own priorities, and their radio equipment was designed with mobility in mind. Disposing of classified material, secret and top-secret files and documents consumes most of his time. The biggest problem is when the volume of material in the burn bag overwhelms the small stove used for normal burning, and in the end he makes a big bonfire.

By midmorning Takeo's ready to say he's packed, loaded, and ready to roll. Things work out conveniently. The bed of the truck he requisitions is loaded to the brim, with just enough room left over to accommodate the suitcases and personal belongings of Generals Ushijimi and Cho, Colonel Harata, four orderlies, three radio operators, and of course his own. Staff personnel must catch their own rides to Mabuni as best they can. There's only room in the truck cab for the driver and himself.

The driver from the motor pool turns out to be a happy-go-lucky sort, not at all impressed with the rank and station of his passenger. "To us drivers it's all just stuff," the man explains. "You got your ammunition, your supplies and your food rations, and then you got your gasoline drums—I hate hauling gasoline—and finally now you got your headquarters files and radio equipment like you got, sir. But it's all just stuff, know what I mean?"

Takeo has to chuckle. The driver isn't being disrespectful—just matter-of-fact. The man's satisfied with his station, and he's good at what he does.

As the morning eases into noon, a chill wind blows in low clouds with misting rain over the Shuri area. It continues and by mid-afternoon it turns into fog covering all of southern Okinawa, conditions perfect to mask the withdrawal. Roads are muddy, but they've been that way anyhow. The advantage the fog provides is it grounds the American little "dragonfly" observation planes that seem always aloft, probing and pushing their nose into whatever they could find going on below.

Precisely at 1500 hours, the convoy pulls out. Next stop will be Mabuni at a cave in a hill beside the southern sea. Truck engines roar to life and make horrendous sounds that carry in the damp air. Engine noise is the one thing Takeo fears, because it can alert the Americans that something is up. Engine noise be damned, they have to get going, and so they roll. Takeo's truck is near the front of the column, and in a matter of minutes Shuri disappears from sight in the rear view mirrors. Progress over the muddy roads and washouts from the rain is agonizingly slow, and they're soon having to order the troops marching south to stand aside.

"If only our luck…," Takeo says and leaves the sentence unfinished.

"It'll hold, sir," the driver states, and kisses a medallion hanging from the knob handle of the engine throttle.

"What's this?" Takeo asks.

"My Saint Christopher's medal."

"You're a Christian?" Takeo says, dumbfounded.

"Hai, domo," the driver states. "Roman Catholic. Anything wrong, sir?"

"No, but it's unusual, wouldn't you say?"

"Not from where I'm from," the driver explains.

"Which is?"

"Nagasaki, sir," the driver answers. "Lots of us from Nagasaki are Catholic. I was christened in the Church when I was a baby. My parents too. My grandparents were the ones who converted."

Takeo smiles—he's just earned a wrinkle. The hours pass torturously slow. Headway is difficult to maintain in this weather, which is now drizzle with spells of intermittent shower. At dusk, partly cloudy turns to gray as dusk. Skies are soon clear, not all that much but enough to be concerned that American light planes, those "dragonflies" of theirs, might be aloft.

The fear is well founded; several of those observation planes are in the air and starting to search. Japanese troops can hear their small engines buzzing above the low hanging clouds. For a while, luck holds; the overcast makes visual observation impossible. Now one dragonfly finds a break in the clouds and reports what he finds. To the Americans it's the final piece to a jigsaw puzzle.

Within minutes American artillery batteries begin illuminating the convoy with an umbrella of star shells. Trucks and troops come under artillery fire, and now even more enemy dragonflies are making slow passes over the Japanese and correcting the fall of shot. Caught in the open with no place to hide, the columns of trucks and slogging foot soldiers haven't a chance; American fire is accurate and devastating.

Takeo's truck is one of the lucky ones; it escapes being hit, but interruptions and stoppages turn the trip into an all-night disastrous experience that seems like it will never end. Road blockages from flaming hulks of trucks come one after another. Bodies of dead soldiers and untended wounded block the road and make progress next to impossible. Somehow their truck makes it unscathed to Mabuni.

Later when he's finally at rest inside his sleeping bag spread out on the dank floor of headquarters cave, he tries to come to grips with the situation. First, General Ushijimi's gamble for undetected withdrawal is lost. Worse, the Americans are aware that the final battle for Okinawa will be fought in the south and that battle is imminent. It's not exhaustion, but a troubled mind that gives him refuge in nightmarish slumber.

21.

Kumiko's Cave

In the firelight of Kumiko's cave, an invading shadow paralyzes everyone. Pandemonium and the wailing of infants alarm Henri and grip Kumiko with fear. The shadow becomes a figure crawling into the red dimness of the firelight to show a face that makes Kumiko's pulse quicken. "You're safe! You're safe!" she bubbles over and over as she runs to throw her arms around Yukichi's neck.

The girls leap to their feet and huddle around their hero, a dismayed Pere Ferrand, who continues to sit and tremble even as he tries to be strong for the children. Now he recognizes Yukichi, and begins shushing the girls, reassuring them they have nothing to fear. The girls relax and run to quiet the wailing infants.

When silence is restored, Henri gets to his feet and steps forward to greet Yukichi who's still locked in embrace with Kumiko. Sudden realization makes him hesitate. The relationship between his ward and Yukichi is more than he was led to believe, and he's still enough of a Frenchman to recognize lovers. A pang comes from knowing what Kumiko left out of her confessions, but he swallows past the lump in his throat and smiles as he extends his hand. "Welcome home, my son."

Surprised, Yukichi withdraws from Kumiko's embrace and starts to bow, but Henri's firm hand restrains him as the priest greets him in the manner of French gai-jins, embracing him and kissing him on both cheeks. Uunable to hide his surprise, even embarrassment by the gesture of friendship, he seeks refuge behind his inscrutable smile. "Domo arrigato, Pere-san," he manages to stammer.

"Come," commands Henri. "Have something to eat. You look terrible, I shouldn't be surprised if you're half starved."

"Hai, Yukichi-san," Kumiko says. "Tabete kudasai. Please eat." As she moves toward the kettle on the fire, she's examining her man, and it's all she can do to keep from shuddering. She agrees with Henri—Yukichi does look terrible. And it's not just his being drenched from the storm, there's a gaunt look about him. For a moment she thinks it's his clothes: none at all on his upper body and an old pair of baggy trousers, tattered and torn and stained. As she looks, she gasps at seeing his healing shoulder wound. Her gasp catches his attention, so he winks with one of those "I'll tell you later" looks they used before he went away. She has to admit, his gaunt look is more thin and lean than the looks of near starvation she's used to seeing in Okinawan refuges.

"I apologize for startling you," Yukichi says. "I called out several times before I decided to enter. My voice must have been overpowered by the storm. Gomen'nasai."

Still smiling, Henri makes a theatrical gesture of clasping his hands over his heart and returns his attention to the suddenly quiet trio of girls clustered around the fire. "Children," he says. "This gentleman is Yukichi Muragaki-san. He is a very dear friend of Kumiko's, and has been away serving as a soldier, but now he is back with us. Please come and introduce yourselves."

Kiyoko giggles and buries her face in her hands, but she gives herself away by smiling through her mask of fingers. Yukichi bows very low and asks her name. This breaks the ice and now the other two girls begin to compete for attention. He laughs, thinking of his coming task of associating names with faces of the young bevy.

When he's able to break free and starting to eat the rice and fish stew Kumiko serves him, he asks her about his mother, father, and two sisters. "I believe they went north in March," she says. "We were going to go there too, but Pere-san—"

"It's my fault, entirely," Henri breaks in, "I'm to blame. The reason we got trapped here in the south was my insistence to stay at the Mission until—"

"Wakari mas—I understand," Yukichi interrupts. "Arrigato, Kumiko, for giving me reason to hope they're safe. I was in the north—taken prisoner and escaped—it's too dangerous for me to have looked for mother even if I had known."

"Your shoulder?" Kumiko asks.

"I was wounded, but they treated it," he says. "I'll tell you everything later."

"By they you mean the Americans?" Henri explores.

"Hai," Yukichi responds. "Right now I'd like to eat instead of talk, if that's all right. I'm hungry; my stomach's empty. Sore wa daijobuda baai. Onaka ga akimoshita. "

"Of course," Kumiko and Henri say in chorus.

As he eats, he's quick to realize they're living on food that pales in comparison with the rations he'd received as a prisoner, but chooses not to mention it. When he finishes eating, he's ready to tell his story. He'll omit any mention of Kozen and how he died, memories too personal to share—even with Kumiko. When he's told his tale, he's ready for questions.

"How in the world did you find us?" Henri asks.

"God must have guided him," Kumiko says.

"Maybe," Yukichi replies. "Mostly it was just luck. I didn't know if you were in the north or the south, but I couldn't stay in the north because it's the American zone, and they would have killed me if they captured me. They shot at me and missed. I'm bound to be a wanted man. There's probably a reward out for me. Anyhow, I stole a small boat and made my way down the coast. I saw hundreds of American ships and boats, but I managed to evade them. The storm helped. I kept going south, asking every civilian if they'd heard of a French gai-jin saishi and his daughter. In Minatoga I got lucky. A fisherman said he'd heard stories about a holy man living in Mabuni. So I started out, asking everyone I met the same question. Then it started raining, and I was on the verge of giving up until tomorrow, when I ran across an old lady who told me about what a gai-jin and his orphans living in what they call the Cave of the Virgins. This had to be it, so I began going from cave to cave until finally I found you."

Henri has a question. "I gather from what you saw in the enemy camp, is it safe to say you think the Americans will defeat the Japanese?"

"Without doubt. Utagai mo naku," Yukichi answers. "I know very little about war, but I saw their war machines and weapons and supplies to know they're far superior to the Japanese. The Americans have enough to be wasteful."

"How much longer until it's over?" Kumiko asks.

"Soon, I fear," Yukichi replies. "The villagers told me rumors about a big battle at Naha and old Shuri Castle. The Americans won and forced the Japanese to retreat."

"Naha?" Kumiko says.

"Totally destroyed, they say," Yukichi answers.

"What else do they say?"

"The villagers are afraid," Yukichi explains. "Their fear is that now the Japanese have come south, there's bound to be more fighting. We're surrounded."

Kumiko gasps and asks, "Is it possible to run?"

"And go where? There's no time and nowhere to go," Yukichi explains. "And we have the children and babies to think of. We have no choice but stay here and wait it out."

"Perhaps the Japanese will see the futility of their situation and surrender," Henri suggests. Kumiko and Yukichi stare at him. Despite years of living among the Nihon-jin, he still doesn't have the slightest understanding of them.

The sound of the night rain outside the cave is like a cataract, and it doesn't let up all through the night and the next day and its night too. Kumiko and Yukichi want to talk. They have words to exchange that can only be said in intimacy, but are forced to sit in silence, daring not to exchange glances that reveal their anxiety. They sit and sleep when they can and wait for the storm to pass.

During the second night, the rain comes to its miserable end, and morning skies greet them with gray clouds while the earth echoes cascading runoff. The air has the smell of springtime as the sun chases the clouds away and makes it a day of vapors. By midmorning calming weather releases the hostages from the cave.

"I've seen a spot overlooking the sea near the top of the hill," Kumiko says. "We can climb up to it and not be disturbed."

"Lead on."

The climb is more of an effort than it appears. First, they have to make their way up from the edge of the sea to the plateau. There, they must ascend a steep path from the base of the hill to the place Kumiko has in mind. They're both winded when they reach the elevated clearing. Their efforts are rewarded by the view—a sunlit panorama of sparkling sea, verdant land, and blue sky with pillows of clouds. Kumiko shivers in the chilly breeze ruffling her hair as she pants to catch her breath. When breathing is no longer labored, she gazes at her lover and smiles at the sight of him. He seems to have no discomfort from the exertion of the climb. What she sees is a handsome face smiling in anticipation for the kiss he's been anticipating since the day he marched off with the Boetai. As he steps forward to embrace her, he's surprised. She turns away and says in a voice soft and full of emotion, "Oh, look. There's a bird."

"Wakari masen—I don't understand," he stammers.

"What don't you understand, Yukichi?" she blurts.

"Us! I don't understand us! You and I—what we are, what we have been. We're lovers, you and I."

"It was wrong," she says. "What we did was wrong. It's a sin."

"A sin? What the hell are you saying? Anata wa ittai nani of itte imasu? How can two people in love commit a sin by having sex?"

"It just is," she declares.

"It's this ridiculous gai-jin religion of your Pere-san is what it is."

"It's not ridiculous! It's my faith."

"Where was your damned faith when you gave yourself to me, when we made love?" he shouts.

"You were going away. I thought you were going to be killed."

"So it was all right to make love with me if I were going to be dead," he argues. "But because I'm alive it's a sin. Is that it?"

"You're twisting my words. I knew I was sinning, but I loved you so much I was willing to commit a sin."

"And now you don't love me anymore. Is that it?"

"I do love you. Only—"

"Only what?"

"I'm going to be a nun," she blurts.

"A nun?"

"Then how can you say you love me?" he asks in his con-fusion.

"It's a different kind of love."

This he ponders for less than a minute. "You know, Ku-miko," he says, "I was going to convert to this gai-jin religion of yours—just to make you happy. We can get married and do all these things your Christian life demands. We can go to Church, attend Mass, support the Church, let you dabble in your religion—"

"Faith isn't like that, Yukichi, dearest," she interrupts.

"Then tell me what it is?"

"For one thing, it's accepting Christ as your Savior."

"I accept him!" he bellows.

"You don't sound like you mean it."

"I can mean it; I can do anything," he counters.

She breathes her exasperation.

"What caused this change?" he asks, getting a grip on his frustration.

"The children," she answers. "I was selfish and didn't want to take them in—at first. And then I found that they needed me. It's a wonderful thing to be needed. I had a revelation, an epiphany. I can't explain it. It just happened. Please try to understand. I want us to be friends, Yukichi—good friends."

Yukichi's brooding silence speaks words. After all he's been through, rejection isn't something he'd anticipated. At this moment he's feeling nothing but the cruel wreckage of life. If he weren't a man, he would weep.

Suddenly they're startled from on high by a tremendous roaring of engines. Overhead in the clearing sky a formation of four American planes appear in a banking maneuver to head in the direction of Itoman. The planes are so low Yukichi sees the silhouettes of the pilots in their canopied cockpits, and one pilot seems to gaze directly at him. Memories coming flooding back of Ie Shima when enemy planes destroyed the bamboo dummies that he and Kozen made, and it produced a longing for his dead friend.

"We shouldn't expose our selves," he suggests. "We should get undercover."

"There's a cave entrance just across the clearing," she says, "There's nobody in it. I found it one day when—"

"Halt! Put your hands in the air," a strange voice interrupts.

Startled, they freeze and stare wide-eyed. Standing before them is a Japanese sentry armed with a rifle aimed right at Yukichi. They raise their hands.

"Stand where you are and state your business," the sentry orders.

"We have no business," Yukichi answers.

"Then what are you doing here? What do you want?"

"We want nothing," Yukichi answers. "My fiancé—the girl here—and I are merely looking. She found it one day some time ago. She didn't think it was occupied."

"Well, it is," the sentry answers, "by the commander of the Imperial Japanese Thirty-second—"

"That will be all, sentry!" a second voice interrupts. "Return to your post."

The sentry wheels, hesitates, and complies as he recognizes a bareheaded officer approaching from the direction of the cave entrance.

"You may put your hands down," the officer says to Yukichi. "And you may instruct your woman that she is free to do likewise."

Yukichi slowly lowers his hands and nods to Kumiko to do as the officer says. When he shifts his gaze back at the officer, he's aware that the officer is wearing glasses and the uniform of somebody important somebody because it not only has the insignia of a major, but also a braided aiguillette.

"The sentry speaks the truth," the officer continues. "This cave is now occupied by the Army for military purposes."

"Please excuse our intrusion," Yukichi says. "We had no way of knowing."

"Yes, of course," the major says, and begins staring at Yukichi's wound. "Your shoulder has had medical attention. I can see where it's been stitched. You two are from the village of Mabuni?"

"No, sir," Yukichi answers. "We are refugees from Naha. We live in a cave at the bottom of this hill."

"I've been given to understand that cave is occupied by a French cleric and a group of children," the major says, easing his hand towards his holstered pistol.

"Hai, domo," Yukichi acknowledges. "This girl is the gai-jin priest's ward."

"I see—and your wound?"

"I was a Boetai guardsman on Ie Shima. I was wounded during the fighting."

"You were with Colonel Udo's northern force?"

"I don't know who the commander was, sir," Yukichi responds. "We mobilized and marched north from Naha to defend Ie Shima. When the enemy attacked, I was wounded and knocked unconscious. I woke up a prisoner in an American hospital."

"We were informed that the entire garrison was annihilated," the major states, looking unconvinced.

"Begging the Major's pardon," Yukichi counters. "There were about two dozen prisoners. I was the only Okinawan. The rest were Nihon-jin."

The major scowls openly.

"We were all wounded, sir. No one surrendered willingly."

"How is it that the Americans let you go?"

"They didn't, sir," Yukichi answers. "I escaped."

"Oh?"

As the officer listens, Yukichi relates his entire experience in the prison camp, omitting only the episode in which the Japanese soldiers refused to commit hara-kiri when ordered to do so. When Yukichi finishes, the major's silent for several seconds and then says, "You have been among the enemy. Tell me what you think of them."

After taking a deep breath and deep thoughts before he answers, Yukichi decides to give an honest opinion to this important officer. "The Americans are extremely well equipped, sir. Their trucks and war machines are powerful and seem to operate well in all weather conditions. Their numbers are too many to count. I believe this gives them an advantage that will be difficult to overcome."

"I see," the major states. "And their soldiers? What do you think of their men?"

"The Americans I saw are very contradictory," Yukichi says. "Some of them show kindness, compassion—one was almost gentle. Yet I have seen some of them turn and be very mean. This is why I say they are contradictory, sir. I believe this makes them the most frightening people in the world."

"You speak as though you believe they are going to win this battle."

"In truth, sir," Yukichi answers. "I believe they will."

"And...?"

"I do not wish to live among them if this is so. Not that they would permit me. They would surely kill me."

At Yukichi's words, Kumiko gasps, earning her stern a look from the major.

"You were once a brave Boetai warrior," the major states to Yukichi. "You still are. Is it your wish to be reassigned to another unit where you can resume your fight with the Americans?"

"I would be proud to do so, sir."

Hearing Yukichi's words, Kumiko's pulse races in her throat. She can't help but wonder what his answer would be if they hadn't argued. Now all she wants is to be alone so she can weep.

22.

Headquarters Cave, Mabuni, 1945

Spring is over. After spring monsoons finish soaking the earth, sunshine and caressing breezes begin turning Okinawa back into the island it was before the battle. Not the sort to ignore how weather, good or bad, affects a battle, Takeo steps outside the entrance of headquarters cave and gazes out over the sunny green vistas of the steep hills surrounding Mabuni. In the outside air, a smell of awakened vegetation verifies the arrival of pleasant weather. Smiling through his despair, he turns his back on this idyllic scene and steps back into the underground headquarters. This change of seasons means trouble. American aircraft are no longer grounded, firm roads assure easy travel for their vehicles, and calm seas offshore allow cargo ships offload supplies and ammunition to take advantage of superior logistic support. One look around is enough to tell him there's no escaping sights of impending defeat. Except for the southern sea, every direction shows tall columns of black smoke billowing skyward like funeral pyres. He sighs, quits woolgathering and heads for the cave entrance. General Ushijimi is waiting for his morning reports.

Not that there's much to report, and what there is of it is bad. It's now obvious that once the Americans took Shuri, they paused just long enough to gas up and go, so now they're advancing in three raging columns, each supported by its own tanks, artillery, and logistics. One final thrust and it will be over; the Thirty-second Imperial Army will be no more.

Taking a cup of morning tea before stepping into the map room, he finds Colonel Harata staring at the map while he holds a crumbled radio messages in his trembling hands. The colonel didn't seem to be aware of his entrance, because he doesn't move, look up, or react in any way, but as Takeo approaches, Harata stirs from his reverie and greets "Konichiwa, Kuroki-san."

"Konichiwa," Takeo answers with a bow.

"I apologize for not seeing you enter," Harata says. "The truth is I didn't notice, but I do welcome your company."

"It's I who should apologize, sir," Takeo says, sorry to be disturbing the colonel when he's obviously pondering something of grave importance.

"No bother, Major," Harata says. "I was just examining the map. It says it all, you know. We're beaten. There's no hope left. It's a pitiful thing to say, but I suppose it has to be said. It's nobody's fault, certainly not our brave soldiers who fought the good fight. We all did. Even General Cho. We did our best; it just wasn't good enough."

Takeo sets his mouth, but says nothing.

"You don't like my assessment? Perhaps you agree with Cho-san that I'm a defeatist. Well, maybe I am."

"No, sir, not at all."

Harata flashes the hint of a smile, and turns back to the map. "So here we are with our backs to the sea," he continues. "Want to see something? Look here at Kunishi Ridge, a near perfect place to defend. I predicted victory here and told General Ushijimi we'd probably win here. We held the high ground; the Americans would have to attack across open plains; and for a while it seemed as though I was correct. General Amamiya's 24th Infantry beat back the Americans time after time. But the enemy is relentless. They captured every approach and keep hammering at us. The problem is, they can replace their losses, but we can't."

"I thought we still held Kunishi," Takeo says.

"We do—for now," Harata explains, fidgeting with the crumbled radio message before continuing. "But when we beat them back, they keep attacking. All they have to do is win once. All we're doing with our little victories is buying time—nothing more."

Leaving the colonel staring at the battle map, Takeo excuses himself and steps into the radio room to check the latest traffic. There's nothing he hasn't seen before. When he returns to the map room he finds Harata-san gone and General Ushijimi now stands alone, his gaze fixed on the map at Kunishi Ridge. Without saying konichi wa, he says "You don't have to brief me, Kuroki-san. Colonel Harata brought me up to date. Any radio traffic I should see?"

"None, sir," Takeo answers, thinking how frail and exhausted his general has become. Weeks underground in this cave is taking its toll on that once lithe, athletic body and transformed him into a sorry figure of a man whose spirit must be preparing to become a ghost.

With a woeful little chuckle, Ushijimi confesses, "Sometimes I can smell the sea up here, and I have this recurring nightmare in which I'm thrown overboard into the ocean. I try to swim, but it's useless. Then I'm tossed onto a shore and barely escape being killed on the reef. When I'm finally on the beach I meet an unseen monster that terrorizes me like I'm a helpless child. Then I awake with a cold sweat soaking my body. What do you think it means, Takeo?"

"I'm afraid I haven't the slightest idea, sir."

"Well, no matter," Ushijimi says. "But what you should know, as sorry a picture as this map is, it isn't up to date. I just received a message from Amamiya-san informing me that he's about to make his final stand. There's no hope. When Kunishi falls, we're all alone. It's almost over."

Takeo lowers his gaze and slowly shakes his head.

"Just think, Takeo, if we were Americans, we could surrender. Would you like to surrender, Major?"

Takeo straightens his posture and glares with hurt feelings.

"No? I didn't think so. You were schooled in the same tradition as General Cho and myself. Bushido! You're a samurai, a student of Zen. Honor means everything. You can't save your life if it means losing face. I'm proud to have served with you. No general could ask for a better aide."

Takeo bows and remains silent, touched by the compliment.

"Let me tell you, Takeo. When I accepted this command, I accepted the fact that Okinawa was as good as lost. I mean to say that it seemed to me that if General Yamashita couldn't win in the Philippines with all the advantages he had, then what chance did I or anyone else have? There's no way Yamashita should have lost that campaign, but he did and you want to know why?"

Takeo nods his answer.

"We haven't lost these campaigns and battles because of strategy and tactics or that our soldiers couldn't measure up. The Imperial Army fields the finest soldiers in the world. Soldiering has nothing to do with it. Logistics! We lose because the Americans have superior logistics. Damn, but that's a bitter pill to swallow—especially for a samurai. What ever happened to bravery, to courage, to honor, to loyalty, to dedication? Gone! Gone! Gone!"

Ushijimi calms his feelings before continuing. "Made in Japan. That's an expression the Americans use to describe a shoddy product. The Americans and the entire West laugh at us, and I'm ashamed to say sometimes I think they're right."

Takeo looks around and notices that Colonel Harata has re-entered the room and stands silently listening to Ushijimi's tirade.

Pausing to light a cigarette, Ushijimi continues. "As a warrior, I have never known defeat. Always I have prepared myself, and the discipline and hardships have paid off. A samurai's first defeat should be his last. This is how it should be, this is how it is, this is the way of Bushido, this is the way of Zen."

"Hear hear," declares Harata-san. "You have expressed what I live by. I am a warrior meant to fight warriors, to meet my enemy in pitched battle on a field of honor. Who first decreed that war must involve women and children, the aged and the helpless? Who commanded the first air raid to fire bomb cities and kill babies too young to know what an enemy is? There has to be a special hell waiting for these bastards."

The two senior officers choose to let Takeo close the discussion. "I must admit, sirs, that I respect and agree with everything you've said. I fervently believe it's better to die here and now on Okinawa than to live and witness the holocaust when the Americans invade Nippon."

Harata nods, but Ushijimi lowers his gaze, and extinguishes his cigarette. It's as though he has something more to say, something he's not yet ready to divulge, something that has to wait for another day.

23.

Kumiko's Cave, Mabuni, 1945

Wailing and sobbing and screaming, Kumiko comes bursting down the path from the high hill, finally throwing her arms about her Pere-san's neck and burying her face in his robed chest. Henri is thunderstruck. He hasn't seen her like this since the night the mission was hit by artillery. Without the slightest idea of where to begin, he realizes he has to wait until she's calm enough to explain the terror. All he can do is put his arms around her and pat her back until she gets control of herself.

"He's going!" she finally blubbers. "And it's my fault."

"Calm yourself, child, and explain. Where's he going and what's your fault?"

"He's going back to the military."

"Oh, dear Lord," Henri blurts.

"He'll be killed, Pere-san. This time for sure. And it's my fault."

Henri lets her draw apart from him and then he sits down, ready to listen, remaining silent as Kumiko tells him of the conversation and events that happened near the cave on the high hill. When she finishes, he ponders before he's ready to speak.

"Friends can become lovers, but lovers can never revert to friends," he explains. "Love's not like that. It's not possible."

Kumiko's face blushes' deep crimson, and she finally says, "Pere-san, how did you know we were lovers? I never told you."

"You didn't have to, child. It's my business to know things about you, even when you don't think I should. I do it because I love you."

"I love you, too," she says. "But I sinned."

"Yes, you did, child. But thanks to Christ Jesus, sins are forgivable."

"I need to remember this."

"Now, are you sure you want to become a novice—and not a wife?"

"I thought you wanted me to be a nun."

"Nothing would please me better, but only if you want it. The most important thing I want for you is your happiness. Novice or wife or whatever, I want you to be happy. This war isn't going to last forever. Peace will come and life will go on. Maybe not like before, but it will go on."

"Pere-san," she states, after musing what she's just thought through. "I'm not confused about what I want. Not any longer. Once I did want to marry Yukichi, but this war changed that. Caring for these children and the babies opened up things I'd never thought about. I admit I made the decision when I thought Yukichi was dead, had been killed in battle."

"And now that he's back...?"

"I still want to be a nun."

"And Yukichi?"

"I love him, Pere-san, but not as a lover. I guess that doesn't make sense, but it's the way I feel."

"It makes perfect sense, cheri."

"Regardless of what I want, I feel guilty. It's my fault he's going away."

"Oui, it is," he agrees. "Yukichi kept himself alive with the love he has for you. He drove himself to return to you, to reclaim what he thought you two had. He's bound to be disappointed."

"He said he'd convert to Christianity for me."

"Oh! Is that the only reason?"

"Yes, he made that clear."

"That's not possible," he explains. "You have to accept Christ Jesus as your Savior because you have faith in Him. It's the only reason. To do it Yukichi's way makes a mockery of faith."

"I tried to tell him that, Pere-san."

They look up and see the approaching presence of Yukichi coming down the path from the high hill, and when he draws close, he hails them.

"I want to say sayonara before I leave," Yukichi says.

"I'm glad that you did," Henri replies.

"Did Kumiko tell you—" Yukichi begins.

"She did," Henri interrupts. "Can we talk about it?"

"No, it's not possible. I gave my word to the major."

"I understand," Henri says. "But what I would like to talk with you is what you told Kumiko about converting to Christianity. I would very much like to discuss—"

"That too is not possible," Yukichi interrupts. "It was a choice I made when I had hope that... But your god is no god of mine, and I don't wish to argue about it. My mind is made up."

"I see," Henri says, giving in.

"Well," Yukichi announces. "It's over and done with, and so I must go."

"Here, dearest one," Kumiko say, stepping forward. Removing her crucifix from around her neck, she places it around Yukichi's.

"But I'm not a Christian," Yukichi manages to stammer.

"Not yet," Kumiko argues. "But maybe someday."

"It was your mother's," he protests.

"I want you to wear it," she says. "Please wear it as a sign of our love, of what we once were. As a remembrance of a silly girl who once was yours, who still loves you and always will in a way that maybe you don't yet understand."

"On that condition, I'll wear it proudly," he says, before turning to leave. Then in tender departure, he leaves them standing there, waving and exchanging their words of sayonara until he gains the top of the rise and disappears from sight.

24.

The note in Yukichi's hand is addressed to Major Yakahama, staff intelligence officer with the 62nd Division. Along with the note Yukichi was given verbal instructions about the safest route to avoid the Americans and get to the 62nd's headquarters. The note is simple and direct, requesting that the bearer be assigned to a combat unit of the old 44th IMB's Boetai contingent.

Upon arriving at headquarters, Yukichi's reaction is anything but what he expected. What he sees is turmoil, seemingly disorganized groups of soldiers shouting at each other without purpose. Only by reaching out and stopping one of the scurrying orderlies does he seize enough attention to be pointed toward a desk where this Major Yakahama sits idly drinking tea. When he finally stands at attention before the major, he finds it hard to believe that Yakahama-san is an officer—the man neither looks nor acts like he knows a thing about what he's supposed to be doing. And when Yukichi presents his note, he sees the major glance first at Kumiko's crucifix before even begin reading it. The major's first reaction is a silly giggle, and he tosses the note back to Yukichi before bellowing, "Sergeant Yawada, front and center!" When an unkempt orderly meanders over Yakahama tells him, "This bakayaro is in a mood to die for his Emperor. Take him to supply and issue him a rifle and enough ammunition to put up a good fight. Then take him up to one of the Boetai units."

"Which one?" Yawada asks.

"Any one. Doesn't matter. They're all going to die. One's as good as another."

Not bothering to salute or acknowledge the order in any way, Sergeant Yawada crooks his finger at Yukichi and leads him out of the continuing turmoil of headquarters.

Away from headquarters Yukichi takes stock of this Yawada-san and doesn't like what he sees. He's a squat, ugly man with bad front teeth that protrude so much that he spits when he speaks, has bad breath, and his uniform reeks of dried urine. "You're a Christian, I see," he hears Yawada remark with a toothed grin.

"Not really," Yukichi answers, reaching up and clutching the crucifix defensively.

"Where'd you get it?"

"From my...," Yukichi answers. "From a lady friend."

"She pretty?"

"I suppose."

"She a Christian?

"Devoutly," Yukichi replies, feeling uncomfortable about where this conversation is leading.

"You fuck her?"

Yukichi blushes and hears the Jap laugh.

"Hey," Yawada says. "Since you're not a Christian, you want to sell the trinket? It looks valuable, but we both know it isn't."

"Iie!"

"Never mind," Yawada says. "I only wanted it for a charm. It never hurts to have as many charms as you can get. For luck, you know. Take me, for instance. I'm Zen, but I also carry some Shinto charms. You can't tell which one will work."

Yukichi turns his head and glares, thinking this man couldn't be real. It's obvious he's a man without faith, so any religion will do.

"Well, did you?"

"Did I what? Wakari masen."

"Fuck her, of course."

Once more Yukichi chooses not to answer.

"You're a surly prick for an Okinawan, aren't you?" Yawada sneers.

Yukichi sets his lower lip. He doesn't want to have anything to do with this man beyond getting him a rifle and leading him to the new Boetai unit.

"Well, I'm waiting," the sergeant says.

"For what?"

"For an answer, you Okinawan asshole. I asked you if you're a surly prick."

"Iie, I am not."

"Good thing. I'd a knocked the hell out of you."

"I was on Ie Shima," Yukichi says, and wishes he hadn't spoken.

"Really? Then why aren't you dead? Did you run?"

"No," Yukichi answers. "I was wounded and captured by the enemy."

"No kidding?" Yawada exclaims. "Yes, I can see the scar on your shoulder. How'd you get away? Did they let you go?"

"I escaped."

"Wow!" Yawada says. "Why'd you come back? You don't want to die, do you?"

"Don't you? I thought all you brave Nihon-jin soldiers fight to the death."

"Unko! Bullshit!" Yawada laughs. "Not me, man. You think I'm crazy?"

"For a Nihon-jin, you're an unusual man."

"Listen, Okinawan," Yawada says, hatching a plan. "You know the land, so let's you and me get out of here while we still can. I've got some food stashed. I've been planning to head north and hide out until this stupid war is over. Then maybe I'll go home. I don't know. The one thing I do know is that I'm not going to get my ass shot off like the rest of these bakayaros. What do you say?"

Yukichi's obvious anger is his answer, displayed without speaking.

"No?" Yawada pouts. "Oh well, I don't need you anyhow. I just thought maybe you'd like to come."

Yukichi remains silent.

"Where's your Christian girlfriend?" Yawada asks.

Yukichi continues his silence.

"Look, you Okinawan prick," Yawada erupts. "I asked you a question. You'd better answer if you know what's good for you, understand? I ought to knock the hell out of you. Now where is she? Not that I give a damn, of course. Okinawan women are too short. I like the tall girls from Hokkaido best. They got big titties. I like titties, don't you? But I guess you haven't fucked any Nihon-jin. They wouldn't like it with an Okinawan."

"Listen to me, you filthy pipsqueak," Yukichi shouts, throwing caution aside. "I don't give a damn who you've fucked or where you go. All I want from you is a rifle and some bullets and my assignment. So give me my rifle and leave me alone."

Yawada stops in his tracks and glares, thinking for an instant he ought to slap Yukichi's face. Instead he laughs and says, "All right, you dedicated bastard. I'll give you a rifle and enough ammunition to get your ass shot off. Then I'll be done with you. Come, we go this way."

Yukichi lets his anger cool before falling in step silently alongside this bakayaro, wanting no more conversation with him.

"Don't mind me, Okinawan," Yawada says. "You've got a right to your privacy. I really don't give a damn. I even admire you for believing in something so much that you're willing to die for it. I just never did."

Yukichi feels the heated indignation go out of him.

"Is your girlfriend really a Christian?" Yawada asks. "What are they like, anyway? I've never know one. The Buddhists pray a lot. Do Christians pray too?"

"She was raised by a gai-jin saishi, a French Catholic. He prays a lot, and I guess she does too," Yukichi explains, irritated at himself for answering.

"No kidding?" Yawada says. "I guess all religious freaks pray—to whatever god they believe in. A lot of them are going to be disappointed, don't you think? I mean, they can't all be right, can they?"

"I suppose," Yukichi agrees.

"Your girl and this holy man," Yawada says. "Are they still in the south? Or did they go north to the American zone."

"The south," Yukichi answers, chastising himself for saying it.

"Hey, that's right," Yawada exclaims. "The note from the big boy's headquarters. From the aide to Ushijimi himself. You came from Mabuni, didn't you?"

Yukichi doesn't answer, struck with the thought that the sergeant isn't as stupid as he appears.

"Didn't you?" Yawada demands.

"Yes, from Mabuni."

"I thought so," Yawada crows. "You leave them there alone?"

"Not alone," Yukichi says. "They have a cave full of orphans. Babies, really."

"A cave full? They've got a cave?"

Yukichi blushes and grits his teeth. This filthy rokude-nashi son-of-a-bitch now knows far more than he needs to know, and the blame is Yukichi's own careless self.

25.

Kumiko's Cave, 1945

"Mama-san spoke to me last night," Kumiko blurts the instant she sees her guardian stir from sleep.

Henri blinks, not sure whether he's hearing Kumiko speak or not. "Did you say something, child?"

"Hai," she answers. "Mama-san spoke to me last night."

"You mean her ghost?" Henri yawns.

"No ghost. Mama-san herself."

"What did she say?" Henri asks.

"She say if we do not go from this place, I will soon sleep with her. She say we all be dead. You too, Pere-san."

"In a dream, you mean?"

"No," Kumiko answers. "Mama-san's ghost came to warn me. She woke me up and told me I had to go. We all have to go. Otherwise we die. All of us."

"Kumiko, it had to be a dream," Henri argues. "There are no such things as ghosts. They don't exist. You must be—"

"Don't tell me! Mama-san did come. I know she appeared. I was not asleep. I was wide awake, like I am now. It was no dream."

"Kumiko, it can't be—"

"She was here!"

"All right, all right." Henri says in a placating voice. "Now tell me, why do you think she wants us to leave? That's what it's all about, no?"

"Pere-san, look around you. The storms are over. The rains are gone. Every day the sun gathers strength. It's summertime outside. We should be out there in the warm sunshine. The children need it. But we stay here in this damp, evil place. Mama-san speaks the truth. We have to go."

Pausing only a pair of seconds before coming to a conclusion, Henri sees the logic behind the story. The aberration might be imaginary, but the reasoning is sound. He understands where she got the idea. It probably comes from the recent crisis when Kanna-yoo developed a fever. The baby would neither eat nor drink. Henri prayed. Kumiko worked and worried and kept cold compresses about the child. Just when they were about to give up hope, the fever broke. So now it makes sense. Ghost or not, there's no denying that it's time to abandon the cave. "Yes, child," he agrees. "You are right. We will go."

"Thank you, Pere-san. Now we have another question."

"Which is?"

"Where?" Kumiko asks. "Where can we go to find safety and security?"

Henri ponders the question and looks up. "Trust!" he declares.

"Trust? What do you mean when you say trust?"

"We have to trust the Americans. It's the only way, don't you see?" he states.

"I don't know," she cautions, recalling the stories she'd heard in Naha before the fighting began.

"We must," Henri explains. "Yukichi told us that some of them are kind. Those are the ones we must find. We'll leave here and follow the beaches north until we find them. Then we'll surrender."

Kumiko shakes her head. "That's all right for you to say, Pere-san. They probably won't harm you because you're a white gai-jin like them. But what about me? And the children? Westerners treat all Orientals alike. I'm frightened."

"This is where the trust comes in, don't you see?" Henri reasoned. "Are you having a change of heart? Just a minute ago you were convinced that we have to go. That's what your mama-san told you, isn't it? We have no other choice—except to stay here and suffer."

Hesitating for only a moment, Kumiko agrees, "All right, Pere-san, we'll trust the Americans. But I have to spend today packing. You, too. We can't be ready before tomorrow morning."

"In the morning will be fine," he agrees. "I wonder if we can still find the cart the Japanese soldier gave us?"

"We burned it for firewood two weeks ago."

"Oh, dear," he says. "How could I have forgotten?"

A smile is Kumiko's silent answer, and now her mind's too busy to planning what to take and what to leave behind. For the remains of the day, she's a scurry of activity, and come sunset she's exhausted. But they're packed and ready to go at first light.

Sleep comes quickly for them all, and it's deep slumber borne from exhaustion. The untended fire flickers and flares until it burns down to glowing embers, barely strong enough to illuminate the dark figure of a stranger invading their cave.

In terror Kumiko awakens! Calculations quick and terrible whirl through her mind, trying to reject the taste of a filthy hand clasping her mouth and nostrils. The primitive part of her brain blocks all thoughts except the need to breathe. An attempt to open her mouth and cry out is futile; the offending hand is too strong, but it relaxes enough to let her inhale and exhale through her nose. She's suddenly aware of the living weight of a body upon her, while she feels her clothing being torn away while another hand is groping her private parts. "My God, I'm being raped!" her mind realizes. She tries to struggle against her body's invasion and finds that arching her back is no defense. She grates her teeth in hate and disgust, but feels electric pain from the driving force of a coarse penis thrusting past her vulva and violating her vagina. She holds her breath until she hears a Japanese voice demand, "Lie still—or I'll kill the others."

Too terrified not to comply, she tenses her body. After enduring clumsy, frenzied movements she feels hot semen spurt into her vagina, and now the hand limiting her breathing mouth moves away to be replaced by dry lips kissing her mouth, bringing a foul, stinking taste and smell, and in that instant she wants to die.

Finally, a body rolls from her while the offending lips release her mouth, and she screams and screams and continues to scream until she has to stop and inhale clean air, even while a Japanese voice laughs in evil satisfaction.

"Merciful Heavens, what's wrong, child?" Henri shouts in the darkness.

"Silence! Chinmoku!" the Japanese voice shouts.

"Kumiko, tell me what's wrong!" Henri demands.

The children stir and add their voices to the sudden pandemonium.

"Everyone be quiet! Shizukani shite," shouts a shrill Japanese voice in the darkness, and now light from a lucifer brings brief illumination until it's replaced by the burning wick of a kerosene lantern. Yellow light fills the cave and reveals the shadow of an unfamiliar creature. Evil stands before them in the form of an ugly Jap soldier standing naked from the waist down, with his half-erect penis hanging down, dripping with satisfaction from Kumiko's wetness. In the dim light, the sight of his conquest brings forth an evil laugh and a grunt of post-copulative pleasure; the Okinawan girl is as beautiful as he imagined.

Kumiko continues to sob, and the sight of her violator renews her intensity even as she struggles to her feet, grabs the remnants of her torn clothing and closes them around her trembling body. Shuddering, she snuggles to stand close to Pere-san and bury her face in his nightclothes as she leans heavily upon his chest.

A flash of awareness of what's just happened grip's Henri's mind, but he ignores every thought beyond that of comforting his ward and tries to keep his voice calm as he pats her back and tells her over and over, "Oh, my poor child, my poor dear child."

"Forgive me, Pere-san, forgive me," she wails.

"Be quiet, bitch!" the Jap soldier shouts. "Shizukana, mainu!"

"Shut your evil mouth!" Henri booms out, his voice edged with hatred he's never before experienced, before returning his attention back to his suffering ward. "You've done nothing that needs forgiving, cheri. The sin is his alone."

Kiyoko is suddenly rushing forward in hysteria and starts pounding the Jap invader with her fists. Yawada reels back a single step, unholsters his pistol and hits the attacking girl across her face with it. A tear in her flesh brings an instant flow of blood. Kiyoko muscles her eyes shut and sucks in air in preparation to cry, and the sound she voices is barely audible.

"Merciful Heavens!" Henri shouts and draws her into him as Kiyoko's tears start to flow, even as her blood soils Henri's nightclothes.

Kumiko stops wailing, rips off what's left of her torn clothing, takes the girl from her guardian, and uses the remnants of her tattered dress to stem the flow of blood as the child clamps her arms in tight embrace around Kumiko's naked body.

Yawada laughs at the bedlam and laughs again at Henri who is now glaring at him and shouting, "May God forgive you. I cannot!"

"Bah! No one needs it, stupid holy man," is the soldier's response before he begins to wave his pistol. "Silence these whimpering akudo."

Henri glares and slowly wins the inner struggle to conquer hatred for this monster. Seeing that Kumiko is tending to Kiyoko, he turns his attention to the rest of the whimpering children and tries to make his voice gentle as he says "Hush, hush, children. It's all right. Everything's all right now. The danger's past."

Slowly the older children stop weeping and huddle close together for mutual support. The two infants stir and gurgle, but do not awaken.

"Stupid Okinawans," the soldier sneers, as he puts on his trousers. "Nihon-jin children do not cry."

"All children cry," Henri counters with disgust. "Now go away and leave us alone. You've obviously had what you came for. Go, I say!"

"How do you know what I've come for, you stupid saishi," the soldier says. "What I came for was so good I'm going to stay for more. I'm moving in."

"Is there no end to your evil?" Henri screams. "Go away! For God's sake go away and leave us alone."

"I don't give a shit for your god," the soldier scoffs. "I ought to kill you, but I won't—not yet. Don't worry about food. I have plenty of provisions. Now I'm sleepy. I'll take the girl's bed. She can sleep on the floor next to me. I'll cradle one of the babies in my arms with point my pistol under her chin, and if anyone tries anything I'll blow her fucking head off. Understand? Wakarimasu ka?"

Henri grows silent, his mind a kaleidoscope of thoughts, fears, and perils. *What additional evil can befall them? Why hadn't he insisted they abandon the cave before Kumiko came to him with her story about her dream? Yet he knows that these things no longer matter. They must persevere through it all. God demands it. What about Yushiko? What about Kumiko? She will have the most difficult ordeal of all. How much more can she take? How much can any of them take?*

26.

Mabuni, 1945

On a breezeless day with an unusual chill in the air, brilliant orange light from the late afternoon sun pours through the cave entrance and casts long shadows. In the gloom Ushijimi sits motionless in cross-legged Lotus position upon the damp earth, his open kimono exposes his bare chest to the cave's cool dampness. Oblivious to the discomfort he reflects upon his life and the man he's made of himself—and the future he'll witness only from the spirit world. At the brink of the great void, it's time to think about death.

How will history books treat him? What they say about the Thirty-second Army? Defeat—certainly. What else? Like a pebble that exposes only a small corner of its mass beneath the surface, it says nothing about its size without digging. Historians will have to dig deep into the details of his battle journals in order to find how he performed. Steps have to be taken to provide future historians with these details. It's the reason he's invited Colonel Harata and Major Kuroki to join him and share the magnificent view on the high ledge at sunset.

"I saw the green spot," Harata states just as the sun dipped below the horizon.

"Did you?" Ushijimi says with a brief smile that runs away from his face. "I often meditate these days. I look for past pleasures. In my mind, I'm once more experiencing Sakura in a Zen garden in the Spring, a fleeting moment of ecstasy when fragrant clouds of cherry blossoms taste the 'White Wind,' and I hear its haunting melody played by a beautiful geisha on a koto."

"You express it beautifully," Harata compliments.

"Arrigato, Harata-san," Ushijimi continues. "I have invited you two here to tell you a story. It's an ancient account set down in Taiheki, the fourteenth century chronicle of Nippon, and it deals with the death of a lowly ranking samurai. The man's name was Shiaku Shimsakon Nyudo, and he was in the service of the last surviving member of the Hojo clan, rulers of Kamakura. It happened that when Lord Hojo's enemies learn that he has grown weak and vulnerable, they decide to make war upon his house. You see, Lord Hojo has no heirs, so his enemies can gain control of Kamakura by defeating him. The enemy's warriors far outnumbers Lord Hojo's small force, so when the attack begins, Nyudo knew for certain that within the hour he and his daimyo would be slain. He writes his death song and then instructs his son Shiro to assist him in committing seppuku in the prescribed manner of Isagi-yoku. Thus Nyudo disembowels himself while Shiro swings his sword and severs his father's head. Shiro now rushes upon his sword and falls dead at his father's feet. Thus ends the Hojo clan, and Kamakura has new rulers."

The story told, Ushijimi sits in silence to allow his guests to reflect about the meaning of the story. Two minutes pass, he looks at them and asks, "Do you understand the story?"

When he sees both nod, he says, "Do you understand why I've chosen this time to tell it to you?"

When once again he sees both guests nod understanding, he states, "Meaning no disrespect, I think not."

As he expects, both Takeo and Mitsuru look up with evident surprise. "Please, may I explain? As you know, to die

Isagi-yoku is the very heart of Bushido, an act dear to every samurai's heart. It means to meet death bravely with a clear conscience and no regrets at leaving life. If seppuku is committed Isagi-yoku, sins and omissions are washed away, and we might even be judged with charity. Every Samurai demands of himself the will to leave this life while still young and strong, like cherry blossoms blown by the wind at the height of beauty—this is the meaning of Sakura."

As expected, Harata and Takeo nod understanding, and Ushijimi says, "Then you understand what it is that General Cho and I must do. As leaders of a defeated army, we know what is expected of us and we will do it soon."

"It is expected of us too, sir," Takeo says.

"Iie!" states Ushijimi. "Not yet. Before you die, you have duties to perform. Let me explain. I'm charging both of you with a task that every spirit who lost its life on Okinawa deserves. Your duty will be to survive this final battle and deliver our battle journals to the IGHQ in Tokyo, so that those who write the modern chronicles of Taiheki will know the truth. After you do this, you are free to follow your conscience."

Takeo thinks to open his mouth in protest, but the stern look he's receiving from Ushijimi brings hesitation and a nod of his head. Ushijimi's expression softens, and the two have unspoken agreement.

"Sir, may I speak—" Harata starts to say.

"Iie!" Ushijimi interrupts. "No discussion about this order. Your duty is to your Emperor, not your conscience. Is this clear?"

Harata lowers his gaze. "Hai, sir. I accept the responsibility."

"Good. That's settled," Ushijimi says, preparing to stand. "Arrigato, gentlemen. You make an old samurai extremely happy."

"Sir, when will… ," Takeo begins. "I mean, may I ask, when will your ceremony take place?"

"Soon, Takeo-san. Very soon."

"Sir, when you perform Isagi-yoku, may my unworthy self be in attendance?"

"I've been counting on it, Major. Will you attend me? With your grandfather's sword, of course."

"Most assuredly, sir. I am honored."

"It's settled," Ushijimi says, clapping his hands. "Now, if you gentlemen will excuse me, I have important matters I must attend to. Sayonara and arrigato for coming."

The two officers quietly take their leave and proceed out of the cave to stand on a grassy flat overlooking the approaches to their hill. Towering cumulus dominate the western sky, but the full moon owns the east all by itself, flooding the land with silvery light. In the distance comes the rattle of rifle fire as American patrols go about mopping up the few remaining pockets of resistance.

"Well?" begins Takeo, feeling as though he should initiate the conversation.

"What's to say? He gave us an order and we accepted. We have a task to perform, and that's all there is to it. I don't like it one bit. It doesn't set well with my conscience, but since it's duty we're honor bound to perform it."

"That's true, sir," Takeo says, thinking he ought not to express his true feelings about the importance Ushijimi attaches to delivering the journals, because after all, defeat is defeat and who gives a damn about how history records it.

"I find this mission incredible, Kuroki-san," Harata states. "Just think, it looks as though you and I will be among the few who emerge from this hell hole alive with our honor intact. Only, somehow it doesn't seem right."

"What's right?"

"Honor's right," Harata replies. "It always is."

"But is this honor?"

"I can't honestly say. Unfortunately, we may not be regarded as honorable men when we get to Tokyo, because Ushijimi's request goes against everything we've been taught. It's a break from the past, you see, but soon everyone in Nippon will probably have to break with the past. That prospect seems frightening."

"Who's to say we'll be there to see it?" Takeo cautions. "Even if we survive this mission, this war is lost. In the coming battle for the homeland, few will survive. And for certain neither you nor I. This mission just delays our deaths, that's all."

"I'm not so sure, Takeo-san," Harata counters. "I'm not particularly a religious man, but I think if Buddha sees fit for us to survive Okinawa, then it may be in his great scheme of things for us to live to see the new Nippon."

"…the new Nippon," Takeo says. "How easily that phrase rolls from the tongue and how very frightening it is to hear it."

"Frightening?" Harata smiles. "Don't underestimate the Nihon-jin, Takeo-san. I can see how Emperor Meiji's ministers may have expressed the same concerns a century ago, and look how much we've accomplished. Whatever changes come, I think our people can handle them. The new Nippon will emerge as an even greater nation."

"Maybe, but I don't think Ushijimi-chan would've wanted to see our new Nippon. He loved the old Nippon dearly and considered it the greatest nation on earth."

"It was, Takeo-san. It was."

27.

Not men to waste time, what little is left, Ushijimi and Cho make the decision to pay the price for failure, and they go about making preparations for their ceremony in the manner of samurai deeply devoted to Isagi-yoku. They'll do it come sunup. As to their bodies, Ushijimi instructs Yoshi-san to scrape out two shallow graves in the grassy hillside and be careful not to mark them with headstones. The orderly understands that his general doesn't want to give the Americans the satisfaction of looking upon his corpse or even his grave. Yoshi-san smiles obedience, and Ushijimi knows it will be done.

One last responsibility is to inform the IGHQ how he's done his duty. The fault for failure is his and his alone. The Imperial Army never abides excuses, so he must be meticulous in choosing his words. Satisfied with the text of his message, he heads to the radio room and hands the message to the radio operator. The man rises and starts to bow, but Ushijimi motions for him to remain seated. "Read it back to me before you send it, dozo," he says.

In words soft-spoken and clear, the operator begins reading aloud. "With a burning desire to crush the enemy, the Thirty-second Army has fought the invaders for three months. Despite our death-defying resistance, we have failed to destroy them. Now we are doomed. Since arriving on Okinawa, our men, in concert with the devoted local population, have done their utmost in building sturdy defenses. After the invasion, our combined air and land forces have done everything possible to defend the island. To my regret, we are no longer able to continue the fight. For this failure, I tender deepest apologies to the Emperor and the Nihon-jin. I pray for the souls of our men valiantly slain in battle and for the propriety of the Imperial Family. Death will not silence the desire of my spirit to continue to serve my country. I am filled with the deepest appreciation for the kindness and cooperation of my superiors and colleges in arms. Now, I bid farewell to you forever. Mitsuru Ushijimi."

With tears welling in his eyes, the operator asks, "Shall I have it encoded, sir?"

"That won't be necessary." Ushijimi smiles. "Send it in the clear."

The operator fires up the transmitter, contacts Tokyo, and sends the message. "Sent and receipted for, sir."

"Well done. Now please write down another message."

The operator grabs paper and pencil, and takes dictation. "To all units still existing of the Thirty-second Imperial Army on Okinawa from Commanding General Mitsuru Ushijimi. For three months you have bravely resisted the vastly superior forces of the arrogant enemy and fought them to a standstill. I congratulate you for performing your assigned mission in a manner that leaves nothing to regret. Unfortunately, organized resistance must now cease. Even so, I urge all survivors to fight to the last and die for the eternal cause of loyalty to the Emperor. May Great Buddha find favor with your spirits."

"Sir, I regret to inform you that we have unfortunately lost radio contact with—" Ushijimi cuts short the operator's apology. "Send it!"

"In the clear, sir?"

"In the clear." Ushijimi bites his lip. "After you send it, shut down your transmitter and guard only for incoming traffic. There will be no further transmissions."

28.

Yaeju-Dake, Okinawa, 1945

A scant fifteen thousand soldiers are all that's left of Ushijimi's once proud army to defend Yaeju-Dake, the last Japanese stronghold on Okinawa. Once they're gone the guns will grow silent. Bound by honor to fight to the finish, the hopelessly outnumbered Japanese have only two things going for them: They hold the high ground, and these hills are a natural defensive barrier.

Thanks to Sergeant Yawada, a slime bag if ever there is one, Yukichi finds nothing but trouble in trying to locate his assigned Boetai unit. After giving the vaguest of directions, the man just ups and disappears leaving Yukichi to fend for himself. He's lost without the slightest idea of where he is or where he's going. Now a night fog comes rolling in from the sea, so he's stumbling around like a drunk in a house of mirrors. The sun sets, the fog thickens, the rocky ground is slippery wet, and Yukichi is stumbling around trying not to lose his footing and tumble down a steep slope. It seems crazy to continue, especially when there's danger of running into sentries on either side and get shot for his effort. The smart thing is to settle down and wait for first light.

He hunkers down in a niche made by the juncture of two coral rocks to spend the rest of this miserable night. Comfort is impossible. With no tunic, there's nothing he can do to ease the chill of the fog on his bare torso, and even Kumiko's crucifix feels cold to his skin. Pangs of hunger gnaw at his stomach, sleep is impossible, so there's little he can do but wile away time and wait for morning.

His mind becomes a jumble of thoughts, of ideas, of memories of poor decisions made under the disappointment of Kumiko's rejection. Regardless, he realizes he'd cast his lot when he told the major at Mabuni he wanted to die. That was rash. But it's going to come about, and probably the only good thing to come of it is to show the Nihon-jin that Okinawans also knew how to die with honor. Comes a remembrance of something his father once said: "It's easy to face danger when there is none, so face danger before you crow, rooster boy."

The memory brings thoughts, *Mother, father, sisters, brother. Are they safe in the north, or dead and buried? No way of knowing. And if by some miracle they're still alive, they'll probably never hear about my death.*

It makes him weep. To escape his inward judgments, he turns to the task of examining his rifle, running his fingers over its action and feeling it in the foggy darkness. All he remembers from the instruction on Ie Shima is that it's .25 caliber, the same one the regular soldiers use, and Yawada took it out of a shipping crate. At the time that toothy Sergeant Yawada issued it to him, he must have been in a generous mood at that time, because he also gave him a canteen, a belt, and a leather cartridge box with ten bullets. Why he hadn't given him a uniform tunic was something.... *Let it go,* he tells himself, and he reaches into his leather cartridge box and started playing with his bullets, until finally he takes one at random and practices loading and unloading his rifle until he's satisfied he knows the procedure. He leaves the rifle loaded and clicks on the safety.

Yukichi is unaware that the chambered bullet is the schoolgirl Naniko's "short round." The first time he fires the rifle the bullet will jam in the barrel; the next round will explode and could blind, maim, or even kill him.

He doesn't remember falling asleep. All he recalls is yawning once or twice and being suddenly aware of morning light. Fog still blankets the ravine he looks down into and could have fallen if he hadn't stopped when he did. From his days on the dredger, he recognizes the fog as the bright gray sort that filters daylight and will burn off by midmorning.

Hunger pangs come again to his growling belly, and to combat the feeling he stretches the stiffness out of his cramped muscles. As he decides to continue his search for the Boetai, he checks his rifle to insure the safety is still on, and it is. He rejects a notion to unload the rifle, but when he thinks about it, he knows that professional soldiers probably wouldn't carry an unloaded rifle, and he decides against it.

After going no more than a hundred meters, he's startled by a challenge of a Japanese voice coming out of the fog. Freezing in his tracks, Yukichi listens until the insistent voice comes again. With fear gripping his mind Yukichi makes a statue of himself trying to recall the words Yawada said were the passwords of the day. "May I have your meishi?" he calls out.

The response is a giggle. "That's not the password," the voice in the fog laughs. "But only a Nihon-jin would ask for a name card in this situation. Come on in."

The voice turns out to belong to a young man, hardly more than a boy with a face too gentle to be a soldier and cast in a smooth skin of excessive oiliness that seems to glow even in the foggy morning light. He smiles and makes ready eye contact, but has no food when Yukichi asks, but he is forthcoming with explicit directions about the best route to join up with the Boetai unit. Yukichi thanks him and parts with a ceremonial bow out of force of habit, and it makes the boy soldier stifle a laugh, which causes Yukichi to blush before he sets off in a brisk pace in the direction he's been given.

The sentry's directions are accurate, so after proceeding no more than two kilometers Yukichi comes upon the most unlikely military unit he could have imagined. Lack of organization sticks out all over the place. They seem to be a small company-sized unit of Okinawan guardsmen, just beginning to break camp when he arrives. True to their ignorance of Imperial Army military discipline, they haven't posted sentries and there's no way to tell who's in charge. He gets the feeling that if he'd been an American, the lot of them would shrug their shoulders and surrender en masse.

It's soon clear he's arrived at both a good time and a bad time. The first thing he's told is that they've received orders to advance and take up positions supporting a Japanese infantry company already dug in along the crest of a nearby ridge. Enemy activity on the defilade of the hill has all the sounds indicating that there will be fighting later in the morning when the fog burns off. This was the good news. The bad news is that he's just missed the morning meal. This comes from a man claiming to the non-com in charge saunters out and greets him. When he tells the non-com how long it's been since he's eaten, the man arranges for some cold rice and hot tea.

The non-com, surprisingly an Okinawan, waits patiently for Yukichi to finish eating, then comes and sits across from him. "I can't help but notice your shoulder wound," the non-com says, "Might I ask, were you in the fighting?"

Yukichi nods.

"I'm Kozo Mojun from Naha," the non-com explains. "I was given the rank of sergeant by a Japanese officer who told me it was because I used to be a bookkeeper on the Shimpo, the Ryukuan daily newspaper."

"My name is Yukichi Muragaki, also from Naha," Yukichi explains, wishing that he might have known Kozo before the war, but he realizes that people working on a dredger and those keeping books for a newspaper probably don't hang together.

"The crucifix?" Kozo explores. "You're Christian?"

"No," Yukichi replies,\. "I wear it because my one-time fiancé asked me to. It's a long story, and I don't like to talk about it."

"Understand, but you're obviously an interesting man," Kozo responds. "Being in the fighting, I mean. You're probably one of a kind. Were you scared?"

"You say that I've been in the fighting, but I don't know that I have. Scared? Yes, we thought we were going to be killed when we were told we were going to attack," Yukichi answers. "Then everything happened so suddenly. We charged, I saw my friend Kozen killed, and I was wounded, knocked unconscious without really being in the battle. I woke up as a prisoner in the enemy's camp. It was strange to have fought someone and never have seen who've you fought. I was given good treatment by some of the enemy, but they have others who are meaner than hell."

"Then you've never killed anyone either?"

"I've never even shot at anybody," Yukichi admits. "All I know is that I was wounded, and I don't even know how that happened."

Kozo gets very quiet, and Yukichi can see he's worried. "Is that what's bothering you? Having to kill, I mean?"

"Yes," Kozo replies. "I don't know if I can do it."

"Only you can answer that."

"I know you're right. I guess I was hoping you could…. Well, you know… ." Kozo says, thinking out loud.

"Kozen did," Yukichi declares.

"Killed somebody?"

"Yes, but it wasn't one of the enemy. It was a Jap sergeant who'd abused him. I saw him shoot the Jap bastard, and I could see that he'd done it to relieve himself of all the bitterness. I think he was almost happy to die."

"You have seen war, I think," Kozo sympathizes.

"So now, this morning, I think I'm going to join my friend."

"You don't have to, you know?"

"Yes, I do," Yukichi affirms. "I have no other choice. After they occupy all of Okinawa, the Americans would hunt me down and kill me. Their interrogators are meaner than the others, but they're the ones who'll be in charge once the battle is over."

"Do you believe in the Spirit World?" Kozo asks.

"I honestly don't know what I believe," Yukichi answers. "Here I am. It's the day of my death, and I don't know what I believe. Doesn't that beat all?"

"Not as much as you might think, Yukichi-san. I'm in the same boat."

Yukichi glances sharply at his new friend. It's comforting to realize that the things troubling him are the same as what's on his own mind.

"Come on," Kozo announces. "It's time to assemble the company and take up our positions at the top of the ridge."

Yukichi falls into step behind Kozo. At that moment he's willing to follow that bookkeeper straight into Hell—and thinks he probably will before the day is over.

Orders come for the Okinawans to form a second line of defense behind the 44th IMB's first line on the heights of Yaeju-Dake. Nothing has changed the minds of the Nihon-jin; despite the dire circumstances, they still don't respect for Okinawans. Digging foxholes is impossible—they haven't any shovels. Fortunately, outcroppings of rocks and undulations of the hillside terrain make natural defenses. They have another disadvantage. From their assigned positions, the Boetai can't see the enemy soldiers as they develop their attack, and it has little to do with the fog bank, which has lifted to make it a sunny day.

Yukichi sees the American assault begin with high drama. From out of nowhere, enemy warplanes are suddenly diving headlong at the 44th IMB's position on the heights. Fiery blossoms of erupting napalm bombs and screaming rockets envelope the crest and its approaches with earsplitting racket. Between waves of attacking planes, Yukichi peers from his cover and sees that fortunately none of the aerial ordnance is targeted on the Boetai. It's the Japs, not the Okinawans, who are catching hell this morning. The aerial bombardment lasts about twenty minutes before it abruptly ceases. Before silence can be restored, a new brand of terror comes. Even as the enemy planes disappear in the distant skies, the enemy wheel out their heavy artillery and start laying down a barrage. As before, the 44th IMB is taking the pounding, while Boetai positions are spared.

When the artillery barrage finally lifts, the rattle of small arms fire comes from the top of the ridge. This phase of battle is the most frightening of all, for it's personal and deliberate with rapid surgical persistence that comes and goes with irregularity. It's soldiers engaged here and there in individual duels, and each goes on until there's no more sounds of rifle fire coming from that direction. When the shooting stops, the silence is eerie and frightening, with the sound of lightly swirling wind blowing nitrate laden smoke with traces of ammonia coming down the slope.

Time goes by without measure. It could be seconds, could be an minutes, there's no telling. All Yukichi knows is the sun being higher, but not at its zenith. He doesn't feel fright, but he's alert and hears only the sound of his pulsing heartbeat. Now there seems to be movement—or the sight of something or somebody moving, but he can't be sure. It could have been a man's head or maybe nothing at all. Another guardsman must be seeing the same thing, for suddenly there's the sound of a shoot. But there's no evidence of a hit and no return fire.

He checks his rifle. The safety is still on—he clicks it off, scared by the sound it makes. He stares intensely, trying to see what is or isn't there or maybe it is, he can't be sure. Pressing the rifle butt firmly against his shoulder like he's been taught, he tries to prepare his mind for combat.

Off to the right, where Kozo is, he hears the crack of a rifle, then another, then moans, then silence, and he somehow knows that Kozo is no more. *I hope he didn't have to kill someone before he was killed himself,* Yukichi thinks to himself. But what he has to face is that the enemy is now attacking his new Boetai unit. He steels himself for the inevitable outcome, which will be his death. He'll try to have courage.

A burst of automatic fire suddenly breaks the silence, but even with this terrifying presence he can't see a thing that's not supposed to be there. Now another burst, and he hears the sound of a moan, then still another burst, and the moaning ceases. Did he see something? Yes, yes he does. He's certain. He aims quickly and jerks the trigger, aware that his eyes are closed as he shoots. He works the rifle bolt, finding it somewhat more difficult than he expects, and smells of pressurized gas as it escapes from the chamber. He loads another round and gets ready to fire again.

Seeing what he thinks is a man's head, he aims and pulls the trigger. He doesn't see the rifle chamber explode, but he feels the shock and when he opens his eyes, his vision is blurred and narrow and dim. He blinks, and suddenly before him is the sight of his worst fear since joining the Boetai.

Standing over him are two enemy soldiers, one with a rifle pointing straight at his chest. He tries to be brave in the face of oblivion, but he cringes as the soldier does not shoot, and suddenly the two are speaking in their strange language he can't understand.

"Shoot the yellow bastard!" he hears the soldier not pointing his rifle at him say.

"I can't."

"Why the hell not?" the other soldier says.

"He's wearing a cross. He's a Christian I can't shoot no Christian. You want him dead, you shoot him."

"Aw, shit! I can't shoot some Jap asshole who ain't shootin' back. We wuzn't trained that way. They's supposed to be shootin' back."

"So, let's take him prisoner. He's our ticket to get off this fucking mountain."

Yukichi's confusion is without bounds.

29.

Motobu, 1945

In the predawn purple, Ushijimi's face is a mask hiding his emotions. "We should have a tolling bell," he says. "Everything would be nicer is we had a bell." And then he flashes a smile as he sees the first orange brilliance of the sun appear on the horizon. "Look, Isamu," he states to his compatriot in this morning ritual. "Heaven honors us with a perfect picture of our flag."

Cho nods and answers with a grunt. Like Ushijimi, he is clad in a white funeral kimono as the two of them stand together side by side before starched ceremonial mats on the ledge of headquarters cave facing into a spanking breeze as they watch the rising sun power its way into a cloudless sky. Tucked into each man's obi sash is a razor sharp seppuku knife.

"Hai, hai," Ushijimi announces, rubbing his hands together as though he is truly happy. "I think we have a splendid morning to do our duty to Nippon, don't you?"

"I've never seen finer," agrees the chief-of-staff as he takes a wide stance with his hands clamped firmly upon his hips while he tries to breathe in courage.

"Nor I," agrees Ushijimi.

"You know, I'm happy to be leaving the stench of this place," Cho says without giving the slightest hint of whether he's referring to Okinawa or to the world.

"I agree," states Ushijimi. "It's time to do what we came here to do."

"My General, would you grant me the honor of preparing the way for you?" Cho asks, having to speak above a noise created by a sudden rush of rising air.

"I would be honored, old friend."

Suddenly they're not alone on the ledge. Takeo, wearing his full dress uniform silently joins them. Conscious of the ceremonial role in which he must do nothing overtly to make his presence known, he breathes deeply and tenses his jaw. His hope is that he's prepared himself to assist in every detail without showing the slightest emotion.

"Major Kuroki-san, are you ready to assist us?" Ushijimi asks, knowing there will be no reply beyond a guttural sound indicating his aide's readiness to use all his strength and skill with his sword to protect them from prolonged pain and make their dispatch to Heaven swift.

While Cho drops to his knees upon the ceremonial mat and stares into the sun, Takeo purifies his sword with a dipper full of water before striding forward to take his position at the ready. With muscles tensed, he draws back his sword and grits his teeth.

Cho takes out his knife and inspects its blade as though he's never looked at it before, and then he fits the point of the blade just below his rib cage. He glances quickly at Ushijimi and announces "I'll be waiting for you beyond the Tori at Yasukuni Shrine."

Takeo takes a deep breath when he sees Cho set his mouth in determination. No outcry from Cho, just performance of his honorable act as he pulls the knife blade into himself, twisting it deep inside his abdomen to feel its purifying pain before his head slumps forward to expose his neck. Takeo sees only a point just forward of Cho's spinal hump and now the sight of the sword's blade invades his vision. The cut is true and deep, and Takeo hears General Ushijimi's grunt of approval as Cho's spirit begins its flight to Yasukuni Gate.

Ushijimi wastes no time. Appreciating Cho's fine example, he kneels and prepares his own ritual while Takeo washes away the drops of Cho's blood from his blade before purifying it again. Fighting back his tears, Takeo strides forward and again takes his position.

Ushijimi glances at Takeo only once, but the look is void of any personal kinship between them as he sets his mouth and then relaxes it. "I only hope the Okinawans won't always resent me for this terrible thing I've brought them," he says just before his seppuku stoke.

Takeo sees his blade strike again with steely effectiveness, and then his vision goes from gray to black to white. When he's conscious of being able to see again, Ushijimi is no more. Takeo takes a step backward and wipes, washes, and sheathes his sword and lets the tears flow. "Now, goddamnit," he shouts. "There are no more lessons for me about how to be a samurai."

After drying his eyes and wiping the tears from his glasses, Takeo takes a stoical stance while listening to the sound of the white silk of the generals' ceremonial robes spanking in the wind, and turns to acknowledge the presence of Colonel Harata who's joined him on the ledge. Before they can say a word, they have to move aside to let Yoshio-san and another orderly claim the generals' bodies and take them through the cave and out into the burial sites. The orderlies work quickly and soon Takeo and Harata are again alone on the ledge. "You saw?" Takeo asks.

"Hai, of course," Harata answers. "I watched from the shadows inside the cave. They performed well. So did you."

"Arrigato, Harata-san."

The two officers grow silent as the minutes pass, each man content to be alone with private thoughts about what they've lost—their general's small victories and big defeats that's led to the destruction of the Thirty-second Army. Startled by the sound of running feet, they move aside to get out of Yushio-san's way as he comes rushing forward to hurl himself off the ledge and fall to his death on the outcropping of rocks at the base of the high hill. Unnerved, Takeo shakes his head. "That's loyalty," he says.

"That it is," Harata concurs. "We should leave within the hour. I've packed the journals and gathered clothes for our disguises. Once we change, we can be on our way."

"I'm not going!"

"Major, you promised! You gave your word."

"Ushijimi-chan was under duress. I'm counting on his spirit to release me from the promise. Besides, one is less conspicuous than two."

"I could order you to go."

"Please don't," Takeo pleads, the hint of threat in his voice.

Harata bites his lip, then accepts the major's decision as final before saying, "I must go. Somebody has to."

They're startled by loud sounds of military activity coming somewhere from the foot of their high hill. "You'd better hurry, Harata-san," Takeo advises. "The Americans are close. They'll be here at any minute."

"Sayonara, Kuroki-san."

"Sayonara, Harata-san. We'll meet at Yasukuni Gate."

"Until Yasukuni," Harata whispers, and he is suddenly gone.

Takeo withdraws his grandfather's sword from its scabbard, looks at the blade, and says to it in bitter soliloquy, "So it's come to this. I am now the entire contingent of the Thirty-second Imperial Army, so come on, old sword, let's go out fighting."

Reincarnation? He wonders if it's true. What will he be? He hopes it's a male child. He laughs at the thought and starts singing a little song from his youth as he turns to stride off the ledge and through the cave to the grassy clearing outside, thinking with every stride that it's going to be a fine day. Grandfather and Ushijimi are waiting for him at Yasukuni Gate, and he doesn't want to be late.

30.

Cave of the Virgins, Motobu, 1945

As good people love goodness, miserable people love misery, and Sergeant Yawada is a miserable man. From the moment he seizes control of the cave, he begins taking delight in dominating these good people. Raping Kumiko is only the beginning; the man seems to have nothing on his mind beyond making life pure Hell for his captives. Perhaps, he thinks, he can show them how stupid it is to have faith in their God.

The only beneficial thing from his coming is his making good his boast of having provisions. True to his word, he delivers a cache of food, so no one will go hungry. Henri is unimpressed. To see his children have nourishment brings minimum thanks.

When Yawada isn't in the mood to fornicate, he thinks up new demands, threats, and torments for his prisoners. In Henri's eyes, the man is totally insane and one day will tire of his evil diversions and kill them all without feeling any remorse whatsoever. The man rarely sleeps, and when he does he leaves orders for no one is to move or talk. To ensure obedience, he sometimes feigns sleep, lying motionless for prolonged periods in hope of trapping them. And when he sleeps or pretends to sleep, he curls up with his arms wrapped around Kanna-yoo while his right hand clutches his pistol with its muzzle tucked under her chin. Yawada has one problem. He snores, so it's easy to tell when he's really asleep.

Still, the sound of his snoring terrifies Kumiko, because when he awakens he's always in the mood for sex. After fornicating he rolls over and snoozes the sleep of the lion, in which he sleeps soundly for a while. These are the times when Kumiko and Henri cam talk, although fear for the children's safety prevents them doing anything else. Kumiko's lamentations are uttered in whispers, and Henri's attempt to console her seems to be words with a hollow ring. But it's his nature to try. "You must have courage, child," he insists. "God knows of your sorrow. Trust in God and take pride in your suffering and fear. God will reward you in Heaven."

"And where is God now that I need Him?" she asks, her face swollen from having shed all of her tears.

"In Heaven, child," he answers. "The same place He was while His Son Christ was being crucified."

Kumiko hears her guardian's words, but she's passed the point where Faith is strong and steady. The life of a martyr is something easier to imagine than endure. She sees Henri blush and convinces herself that maybe her guardian is beginning to find his words difficult to believe. She turns her face away and smirks as he prays, "Give us strength, Oh Lord. Deliver us from this evil."

"Give us strength, you say?" Kumiko sneers. "Always you say the same things, Pere-san. What good is God if He refuses to help when we need it the most?"

"I—" Henri begins.

"Haven't we prayed for help over and over and over, and what becomes of it? How can you continue to say the same old prayers? Tell me!"

"I say them because I truly believe. The good is in believing that God will grant us Salvation for our souls. Nothing else. He grants us nothing else."

"Why?" she asks. "Why nothing else? Any god who lets his believers suffer like he lets me suffer doesn't deserve to be god any longer. That's the way I look at it."

"This is Satan's doing. He wants us to suffer."

"Satan?"

"Yes, Satan. Without Satan, the world would have no need for Christianity. Satan knows this, and so his greatest trick is convincing the world he doesn't exist. But he does and he has people like Yawada do his evil."

"It's all a sham, Pere-san. It has to be! Who needs a God who only sits in Heaven and lets all sorts of evil and horrible things happen, and not only to me, but to the entire world? There's no God, no Satan, just the world as it is, and nothing more."

Henri purses his lips and looks away for an instant, far from abandoning the argument because it's now obvious he's arguing for the soul of a woman he's raised from a child, and he's not about to give in. It's like he's arguing with Satan himself who's taken control of Kumiko's mind and is speaking through her.

"The evil men are right," she continues. "Your god is nothing more than silly superstition, a myth conjured up in the minds of stupid old men. All you do is talk. You never do anything to help yourself."

"Hush!" Henri commands. "Don't blaspheme. The Lord is all powerful. And yes, God could intervene if He chose to do so. When He doesn't, it's because it doesn't serve His greater purpose."

"Greater purpose?" she shrieks, not caring if she might awaken Yawada. "Tell me, Pere-san, what is this almighty purpose? Just what purpose could be greater than the deaths and destruction of millions of people? This is something I can't understand and certainly not accept."

"God hasn't revealed it to us yet," he argues. "We must be patient. Remember, God promises Salvation for our souls, not glorification of our lives."

"I'm not concerned about my life," she cries in her hysteria. "I'm talking about my mind. Can't you understand what's happening to me? Can't God? I no longer care about my filthy body that's been turned into a pleasure vessel for this—this beast!"

Despite her outcry, the sleeping sergeant is not aroused from his slumber. He continues to snore with his hand clutching his pistol.

"Quiet, child," Henri warns. "You'll wake him."

"I don't care," she wails. "Let him wake up and kill me. He's already killed me inside. What more can he do?"

Kumiko buries her face in her hands and sobs in heaves. Henri reaches out to comfort her, but she flings his arms away. "Look, Pere-san," she continues after regaining composure. "Do you want to know why we all stay alive? Do I really have to explain why he hasn't already killed you and the children?"

"Tell me, child."

"Because of me," she says. "He wants my filthy body. He wants to sleep and awaken and have sex, and then he struts around striking terror into us until he gets in the mood to have sex again."

Henri lowers his gaze, stares at the floor, and wrings his hands.

"Don't you realize that I'd rather kill myself than to let him have his way with me? He knows it, and so we struck a bargain. He leaves you and the girls alone, and I agree to be his woman. I bargained to be his whore—his whore! Can't you see how I hate myself? I give this ugly evil Jap everything that I denied Yukichi so that you and the children might live. And you dare tell me that this suits God's great purpose! Has God ever done as much for you? And then in the next breath you're telling me that his almighty purpose hasn't yet been revealed. Yukichi is probably dead, I'm a whore, and thousands upon thousands of our people are dead or starving, and you say it's for some great, unrevealed purpose."

"Oh, Kumiko," Henri wails. "Have I failed you? Haven't I taught you that the greatest gift in life is Salvation?"

"You've tried, Pere-san. I just can't see it," Kumiko laments.

"God is with you, with us. Who can defeat us?" Henri counters.

"Who is to say God is with us? Isn't it obvious that he's not?"

"Even if that were so, and it's not, " Henri answers. "I am with Him; je suis avec Lui. C'est ma facon, c'est ma voeu, c'est ma vie!"

"Few people have your faith," she shouts. "Certainly not I. Can't you see, there is no purpose? There is no God. Evil is all there is. I'm so miserable I want to die. Help me! Please help me! I want peace. I want justice. I don't need words."

Henri reels, feeling lightheadedness at first, now a cold sweat with a ringing in his ears, until his arms grow numb. He stands and fights to stay upright, and staggers several steps before catching his balance. Losing the strength to continue standing, he sits down in a heap to keep from falling. After moments that seem meaningless, the lightheadedness goes away and awareness returns.

"Pere-san, are you all right?" Kumiko shrieks.

Henri nods and looks wide eyed at Yawada, who's starting to stir from his sleep, his pistol still clutched in his grip.

In the next instant, the cave fills with sound. A loud-speaker is suddenly blaring from outside the cave entrance.

The voice speaks in Japanese, the most beautiful and perfectly spoken Japanese they've ever heard.

"Attention," the beautiful voice declares. "Attention soldiers or civilians occupying this cave. Come out! You will be well treated. We mean you no harm. You must come out. You will be given food and care. Medical treatment will be provided if you need it. Abandon your cave! You must come out."

Sergeant Yawada is instantly awake. "What's happening?" he demands.

The loudspeaker blares again, repeating its message. Yawada listens, and when the message concludes and commences again, he's of a mind that he knows what this is all about. He scowls and waves the pistol at Henri and Kumiko. "Keep quiet!" he whispers hoarsely. "Stay still. They'll go away."

The loudspeaker message changes for the next spiel. "Listen, all you people inside the cave," the beautiful voice blares. "Come out with your hands raised. You must come out. We will not harm you. But you are in danger. We will wait ten minutes, and then we are going to blow up the cave. Do you understand? Come out. We are going to blow up the cave."

Panic seizes the cave occupants. Even Sergeant Yawada seems as though he might be starting to lose nerve, but he shushes the others and glares at the cave entrance.

"We have no choice," Henri pleads. "We must go out.

"No! Iie!" Yawada proclaims, pointing his pistol at the priest. "Don't anybody move. They're bluffing. They'll go away. They're not really going to blow up the cave. Everybody sit still."

During the minute, the loudspeaker repeats its message three times as before, and grows silent. Minutes pass before the next announcement. "Five minutes. You now have only five minutes! Please come out! We don't want to harm you. Come out."

"Can't you see, man, they're not bluffing?" Henri screams at Yawada. "They're really going to blow up this cave."

"I said iie! They're bluffing, I tell you."

"Please," Kumiko pleads. "For the children's sake."

"Never! And keep those damned children quiet."

"Four minutes," the loudspeaker blares. "You have only four minutes. Come out."

"Man, they're going to do it. Please let us go," Henri pleads.

"Iie, I say. They're going to go away. You'll see."

"They're not!"

"Quiet!"

"Three minutes," the loudspeaker blares. "You have only three minutes to come out, then we're going to blow up the cave."

"At least let us go. Please let us go," Kumiko begs. "We promise not to tell them you're here."

"No!"

"Let the children go. What harm can they do?"

"I tell you, they're bluffing."

"They're not!"

"They are!"

"Two minutes," the loudspeaker blares. "You now have only two minutes to come out before we blow up the cave."

Yawada grunts, trying to remain resolute in what he's convinced is an American bluff. Whatever doubt might be creeping into his mind he quickly extinguishes. He bites his lip and steels himself. He has to be right. Regardless, he's not going out, and neither is anyone else.

"One minute, the loudspeaker announces. "One minute until we blow up the cave. You must come out. Please come out. You will be safe, but you must come out now!"

Henri looks pleadingly at Yawada, but the sergeant points his pistol at him in silent reply. The seconds tick by.

"This is your last chance," the loudspeaker with the beautiful voice declares, "Come out! We're going to blow up the cave."

"Don't shoot!" Henri shrieks as he scoops up Kanna-yoo and bolts for the cave entrance. Kumiko and the children scream, Yawada fires his pistol, the sound deafening in the cave. The bullet strikes Henri in the back and propels him forward through the cave entrance, where he loses feeling and shouts, "Domini, c'est fini!"

The instant his body tumbles forward into the sunlight, a satchel charge of TNT is hurled into the cave. Kumiko screams and reaches for the children. Sergeant Yawada pisses his pants. The fuse hisses, smokes, and detonates the explosives.

All inside the cave cease to be.

Epilogue

Okinawa, 2013

On a brisk day in late February of 2013, a prince of the Roman Catholic Church stands on a precipice of southern Okinawa overlooking the South China Sea and stares at the scarred shoreline where there's a grotto the locals call Cave of the Virgins. The cold sea wind makes Cardinal Yukichi Muragaki shiver as he holds a small crucifix in his trembling hands and recalls how it's influenced his life. Lost in reverie, he's almost forgotten that a chauffer sits waiting in a limousine to drive him the to Naha airport to catch a plane to Rome where he'll meet with the College of Cardinals and elect a new Pope. He's been in the Vatican only once before, when he received his red cap.

Yukichi's mind isn't as keen as it was sixty-eight years ago, but he still has to deal with memories of those terrible times when the world had gone mad in the Great Asian War. Throughout his years, the continuing thing that's puzzled him is that those who should have lived, died; while those who should have died, lived. And only God knows why. He says a little prayer, smiles at his good memories, puts the bad ones out of mind, and turns to go. He has a plane to catch and a Pope to elect.

END

About the Author

John Wells is a retired naval engineer living in Annapolis, Maryland. A graduate of the U.S. Naval Academy and the Naval Postgraduate School, Monterey, California, he cut his teeth by writing technical documents for Navy shipbuilding programs that resulted in his ability to express ideas clearly and elegantly, but it's been a lifelong obsession with classical literature that honed his skill to become a professional wordsmith who writes fiction that has readability and character-based dynamic storylines. A literary realist, he has developed a writing style suited to modern readers in this publishing era when novels have to compete with television and video games. He believes that "following the crowd" in writing guarantees mediocrity.

www.ingramcontent.com/pod-product-compliance
Lightning Source LLC
Chambersburg PA
CBHW020403030726
47496CB00007B/2271